Thank you very much for purchasing this book.

Title Unleashed
Subtitle: Werewolf Romance Novel
Author: Rose Charles

Table of Contents

Unleashed

Description

United for the sake of peace, divided for the sake of peace. Humans and werewolves do not share cities, let alone hearts.

Samantha Binds

A moderately successful interior designer from Green Bay, Succor City, Alabama, Samantha believes she lacks focus in life, and has recently began wondering if she had been searching for it in the wrong places, most notably in her less than satisfying relationships with men who seem to take more than they give. She is more than ready to give up this aspect of her life, but then, won't the chasm be too great and deep for her to fill it alone? She is afraid of finding out.

She is sauntering home alone from a night party when she rescues, apparently, a man from a pack of dogs. Despite the fact that he is injured and shaken and her current mood is nothing to be celebrated, she is not oblivious of his rippling muscles bulging through a tattered shirt, and his blatant masculinity evidenced by a well chiseled face, thick stubble, expressive eyebrows and deep-set eyes that seem to probe into her very soul. He towers over her as he tries to assure her in a deep voice, deeper than she's ever heard on any man, that he is fine.

He brusquely brushes her off when she expresses concern and suggestions of a hospital, but she is undeterred by his rough exterior, for this may be her only chance. She is willing to break centuries old prohibitions. At a time when humans and werewolves share the world but not cities, Sam wonders if casting her net wider would not be a better option. He may be just what she needs to focus, to make her forget Nelson Cheep, her stingy, cheating boyfriend.

Even if it is only for one night.
***

Kane Limaric

He has a past he wishes gone, a present he can barely tolerate and a future he dares not glimpse into. Five human bodies have been discovered in the Leeve Valley which divides humans and werewolves, and all evidence points to Kane.

It is a crime for a werewolf to maim, hunt and/or kill humans. Before he could be brought before the Council of Ethics for a trial and possibly a death sentence, he escapes. Now an outcast from his community, Kane must live in the human world masquerading as a human. It seems he's been found... but he'll go down fighting...

More than his werewolf primal instincts are awakened by the human woman who interrupts the fight he would rather forget, for at the back of his mind he knows; if she had not appeared when she did, he would be dead.

He knows the centuries old peace rules. He disregards them and chooses to break them by burying such thoughts deep in his subconscious as he follows the woman who seems eager to tear away what remains of his clothes. He mistrusts humans and especially ones who ignite his desires to a scorching heat that incinerates his past... making him forget it even if for a short while...

However, he will be forced to face his demons once again when like the mythical phoenix; his past reawakens from the ashes of his passions. Will he face it and prove his innocence or will he run again?

Fate or destiny, it is up to the two, a werewolf and a human to find out as events precipitated by their chance meeting unfold and spill out of control.

Chapter 1

"Why don't you just dump him if you loathe him that much?" M'lyka asked. They were sitting outside their favorite coffee place, under a young Jacaranda tree. A large umbrella shaded them from the tree's purple flowers which showered their surroundings with every passing of the afternoon breeze. Sam stared at a just fallen flower as she mulled over M'lyka's question. She seemed to be feeling sorry for the just detached petal from its parent tree, and as she stared at it, she felt a strong urge to console with it due to the fact that it would never be with its parent again. The feeling sent a slight shiver through her, which M'lyka noticed.

"You chilly?" she asked, expressing genuine concern through her dark eyes, "It seems awfully windy here. We can move over there..."

"I'm fine," Sam assured her, "I'm just shivering from all my past mistakes."

"Sam," M'lyka remonstrated, "Don't beat yourself so much. I know I asked you out here to talk, but don't carry all the blame." Samantha looked at her friend and felt a tenderness she couldn't express with words wash over her. The only way to express it, it seemed was through the tears that filled her eyes and the emotions that heaved within her.

M'lyka Bose had been in Samantha's life for as long as the two could remember, and the two shared the sort of friendship that seems to have weathered every impossibility flung its way. Through wet eyes, Samantha observed her friend, experiencing a deeply genuine affection which her friend picked up wordlessly, and the two shared a silent moment.

"Do you feel sorry for flowers?" Breaking their affectionate gazes, Samantha turned her attention to the still raining Jacaranda petals. M'lyka did not betray any reaction the sudden question may have had on her. She looked about them at the purple flowers lying around, some bruised, and others wilted, but most still fresh from their detachment from the parent tree.

"Um, they must be shed if the tree is to bear seeds, I understand," she answered her friend, then stood up and looking around, bent to pick a petal. She placed it on the table and they both tuned their focus on it. Anyone observing them from afar may have wondered what held their interest so much. Sam picked up the flower and placed it delicately in her hand. She sniffed it gingerly then turned it over slowly.

"Imagine if the tree stuck to its flowers, then it would not be able to move on and start afresh," M'lyka spoke philosophically, "to progress, to heal, we let go and from the pain carry as much experience... Look out! A bee!" she screeched suddenly and Sam reacted instinctively, more from her friend's cry than the words themselves.

She dropped the flower suddenly without even knowing why, only to notice a small bee extricate itself from the now bruised petals and buzz away.

"I'm not ready to mop the tears yet," she said quietly without looking at her friend.

"You will have to, sooner or later," M'lyka took her hand across the table and grasped it, "But then once free you'll have a chance to start all over again."

"You know, M'lyka, I can't pretend that I feel fine," Sam spoke up suddenly, and M'lyka nodded, "Before breaking up with him I'll have my revenge! I'll let him find out about it! I'll make him feel how I feel- or even worse..!" she seemed animated with every word, and M'lyka registered mild concern which turned more serious with every word Sam blurted.

"I'll find out if he has friends - M'lyka, I got it! He'll find out, that cheating bastard and then I'll have had my revenge!" she drew in a sharp breath and smiled. M'lyka did not.

"Sam... what if he finds out?" she asked with a voice full of concern.

"It's payback, remember?" Sam sneered, "I caught him with Jennifer. Time he caught me with one of his friends!"

"Sam..." M'lyka tried again, but Sam, already consumed with her new idea brushed her off.

"You don't have to say anything at the moment, M'lyka," she waved her hand. She had an unpleasant gleam in her eyes. M'lyka sighed with worry for she knew - once consumed by an idea, no matter how wild or risky, it was next to impossible to dissuade Sam from seeing it through. M'lyka was yet to get used to her friend's sometimes reckless deeds. At times, all she could do was to stick around and provide an ear for the venting that was bound to follow the failure of some of such ventures. Her heavy sighs were enough signals to Sam that she was free to do what she was bent on doing, consequences later.

"I can already see the look on his face!" Sam shook her clenched fist in a victory she was yet to claim. "He had the audacity to sleep with Jennifer and then come crawling for forgiveness!" Suddenly, she grabbed the edge of the table with both hands and leaned forward, as if about to reveal a secret. M'lyka leaned forward too.

"He's never paid for a single meal the entire time we've been going out!" Sam whispered loudly. "Cheap Cheep!"

"Oh," exclaimed M'lyka. "Isn't Jennifer stingy as well?"

Sam shrugged, "They ripped each other off," she laughed. "They deserve each other."

"Didn't he tell you they were just kissing?" M'lyka asked. She tried to maintain a quieter demeanor in an effort to bring Sam lower from her heights of grandeur. It was working, though Sam still sounded gleeful as the nasty gleam faded from her eyes.

"Who knows what else they have been doing? I wasn't in the mood to find out if what he claimed was true or not. Fact is that they were in bed, together."

"You've been blowing him off since then?" M'lyka, sounding relieved, asked.

"Yes, giving him a cold shoulder. He's tried to apologize...but," Samantha shrugged, "don't they all when caught?"

***

The subject of relationships and inept partners was still in their minds and on their lips when they left Melanie's Coffee.

"He called this morning- wants us to 'talk'. He tried to invite himself over tonight, but," Samantha shook her head firmly, "I'm having none of it."

"He'll come anyway," M'lyka mused. "He'll call, you'll listen, you'll think 'perhaps there's a chance at making it work' kind of thing- you know how it is."

"You've truly mastered my life," Samantha glanced at her friend, "while I'm yet to understand a single thing about you. Why are artists so mysterious?"

"They are not- we are not. You are an artist too, Sam. Don't you give spaces that decorative touch?"

"It's not the same, M, let's be honest. Sure, I decide what goes well with that type of ceiling, what is the best carpet for French windows, but..." she trailed off.

"But what? Is my work any different?" M'lyka asked.

"My God, it is! Looking at a clear canvas, then splattering paint all over it, and the result turns out better than the actual subject- tell me that is easy."

"It is easy."

"It is not, and you know it M'lyka. Translating something from your mind using paint..."

"Well, and I can't begin to fathom what having a couch that matches with a cooking pan means, and yet, clients are willing to pay for just that," she grinned. "Please tell me you don't make some of it up."

"I went to school for it, M'lyka," Samantha defended her profession. "But you already know that, you pushed me into pursuing it."

"Yeah I did," M'lyka smiled with feeling. "You've always been good with designing- remember pointing out what you called shoddy decorations..."

Samantha laughed. "Yeah, whenever we visited any of our friends! I would end up redesigning their rooms."

"Your obsession to redefine a room or any space using colors and shapes seemed to border on some form of OCD. That's why I suggested you pursue interior designing as a profession."

"Uh, what?" Sam peered at the rearview mirror. Her attention wasn't immune to the silver Dorado that was weaving in and out of traffic.

"He has been tailing us for the last ten minutes." M'lyka spoke up, nonplussed. Samantha glanced at her, then back at the rearview mirror.

"You've been quiet about it this whole time?" she scowled at her friend.

"I wasn't about to ruin the moment we've just had," M'lyka stated firmly. "We needed it."

Samantha nodded slightly, though her glance kept reverting to the vehicle behind them. She knew it was Nelson Cheep, the man she was trying to stay away from. Couldn't he stay away?

"I wouldn't mind-" M'lyka started, but Samantha cut her off,

"The creep is trailing us." she sounded irritated at that fact, "Now he's three cars behind us."

M'lyka turned in her seat and squinted at the rear window. She turned back around slowly. "I really don't know why you're avoiding him. Just tell him you're... well, how long has it been? Three months? Two?"

Samantha remained quiet, but her mind was not. In a moment, it had transported her back three months or thereabouts, when she had first met Nelson Cheep, the man she no longer wanted to be with. It had been a hot, humid morning.

The seated man looked up as she approached the reception. Samantha glanced at M'lyka, who had summoned her from her office, impatiently. M'lyka just shrugged slightly as if saying *I couldn't help it, he just asked to see you.* Sam approached and as she observed the sitting man, she felt the familiar irritation rising from deep within her. She hated early morning interruptions.

She had woken up late with a nagging stomach upset, she had barely made it to an appointment with a potential client, and just moments after arriving at her office, M'lyka huffs in, scruffy-looking man in tow. All these were enough ingredients to sour up her whole day. She wasn't ready for it.

Samantha highly disapproved of walk-in clients. They wasted one's time and half the time never gave one the job, after hours of incessant haggling and parring over prices. Another pesky client, she thought. He had refused to step into her office according to M'lyka, preferring to meet Samantha out in the reception area. Perhaps he wasn't a client after all. A besotted stalker perhaps?

She glanced at the man briefly. This was no client, potential or otherwise, she deduced. Even seated, she could tell that he was tall. His dark eyes looked back at her, and for a fleeting moment, Samantha had an eerie feeling that those black eyes could read her mind. She stared him back, mentally willing him to back down. He did not. Deciding not to be the one to lose, Samantha stepped closer without breaking the gaze. The seated man held it without blinking. The challenge was on.

"Ahem..! Sam, this is..." M'lyka, sensing Sam's foul demeanor, stammered.

"What does he want?" Sam cut M'lyka off rudely.

"He says..."

"I'll tell her," the seated man added his voice.

In an unbelievably short moment, several things happened to and around Samantha. The rain whipped the window panes with more fury. The lights blinked twice and went out. M'lyka cursed loudly and coughed at the same time. Parson, Samantha's young receptionist, swooned dramatically. A moment of slight confusion reigned, and more so to Samantha.

She felt lost for a moment, wondering where she was and whether she really belonged there. All the while her hazel eyes never left the seated man's dark ones. Not even when he started to rise from his seat.

Samantha watched in wonder as the lean flame unfolded. Too late she realized she had broken her gaze to gawk at his long limbs and wide shoulders. When she looked back at his eyes, they were still boring into her, reading her, probing her thoughts, perhaps even drawing her out... he walked around the table and approached her. Samantha took two steps closer. To her right, M'lyka let out another politely irritating cough which seemed to say, 'Please Sam, don't let out your temper on this masterpiece of physical perfection.'

That was just what the man was. Used to appraising interior decor, Samantha took note of his torso, wide at the shoulders which extended into two muscular arms, and set proportionately on two long legs. The legs had stopped striding and were just a few inches from her. She looked up. The black eyes were still on hers.

"You hit an animal with your car," the thin lips parted, formed the words, and the deep voice let them out. Samantha could only stare. This is a masterpiece of perfection, she thought as she ravaged him with her eyes. Her blatant gawking did not seem to faze the tall man though. Samantha felt herself drawn further into his stare.

"Ahem!" M'lyka ruined the moment. Samantha craned her neck to look up and she took a few steps backwards to better stare back at the dark, seemingly blazing orbs.

"Did I?" she felt herself croon.

"You did. Were you not the one speeding recklessly at six in the morning?"

"Speeding recklessly?"

"Were you not on the East Road..." one long leg was shifted to change his standing posture, and looking down, Samantha noted that he had on open shoes. She counted the toes. She heard a strong yearning to touch them - provided they don't stink, she thought. Suddenly she wondered if any part of him emitted any foul fumes.

"...hit the animal." He was still speaking, but Samantha barely heard most of what he was saying.

"I don't recall hitting any animal."

"All the same you did. Your car carries the evidence..."

"It was dark, Mr..!"

"Nelson..."

"...and I wasn't out there to keep an eye out on every critter crawling and scurrying all over the road! What do you want me to do? Raise it back to life?"

Nelson had been about to say something, but he pressed his lips shut the moment those words were out of Samantha's mouth. Even M'lyka gasped in the shadows, for the power was yet to return. Nelson turned to M'lyka, his dark eyes telling her to speak some sense into her friend.

"Sam..." M'lyka whined in that placating voice that carried with it sincere warning.

"He accused me of something I'm not aware of." Sam retorted

"He only wanted to..." M'lyka started just as a blinding flash illuminated the whole room. A loud clap of thunder cracked outside, and the storm let up. In less than a minute, the sun was out. Samantha felt her temper deflate as she looked out the window. She turned to Nelson,

"I'm sorry," she said it simply, without elaboration, without letting on anything through her eyes. The tall man nodded.

"That is all I wanted." He turned to leave. Samantha felt as if some part of her- a piece she had just discovered she had- was about to stride out with the fascinating marvel of perfection now headed for the front door, which M'lyka now held open.

One thing Samantha had always prided herself in was the fact that she could control her impetuousness ... always thinking through things before taking action- but something failed her this wet but sunny afternoon. She felt her every motion and heard her words as they left her lips, slowly,

"Mr. Nelson?" She approached him and he turned to look at her. His hand was already on the open door. Samantha looked up at him as he reciprocated her gaze. Suddenly and overwhelmingly so- just at that moment when time respects such incidents by stopping- she realized that she was a woman and Nelson was a man.

She had known from the moment she had met him, but now she sensed it, and the realization made her gasp. Standing as close as possible and feeling glad that she had let loose her dark mane, she looked up at the dark eyed man and let the words out.

"I'll buy you lunch."

Nelson looked at her a moment before answering, then did. He walked out the door. Sam looked on as he avoided sparkling puddles - and she sighed sadly. He had taken with him that part of her she had just discovered she had. His answer to her question had just confirmed it.

She remained where she was, watching the steaming, wet ground outside and the few trees shake their leaves gently in the afternoon breeze. Their waving shed drops of water, and the sight mesmerized her. She wanted to be outside. She wanted to walk around sparkling puddles.

She wished to stand under trees that shed grateful tears after a storm, and by her side, she yearned for her stolen part- no, not that, she decided. She wanted whoever had taken that piece of her to be always by her side.

Three hours later, Samantha met Nelson Cheep, but under very different circumstances this time.

"I don't mind Samantha. As long as you are sure you're okay, then I'm okay too. The deed is done, we can now move on," he smiled, and Samantha could have tackled him there and then, such was how urgently she wanted him. At the back of her mind was that constant nag that this was too soon, you barely know him, what if he is a psycho... she shook her head to evict the thoughts.

"You were mad, Sam." He leaned towards her and held out his hand. "I know we've just met but, I mind. I didn't mean to upset you with such accusations."

She gave him her hand and felt him slip it into his, and covering it with his other one, looked into her hazel eyes. She regarded him back, and the communication was silently passed. Even as they stood up, hand in hand and walked into the night, the small, nagging voice in her head would not shut up. In the parking lot, she looked about in the artificial light, and indeed, just as she had suspected, there was M'lyka's dark Honda, parked beneath an uncomplaining Tulip tree.

Sam smiled slightly and held Nelson's hand tighter. Feeling her eyes well up emotionally as her mind prepared her psychologically for the night ahead, she tugged at his hand and he paused. He looked at her upturned face and in answer to her silent yearning, leaned closer to give her a taste of it all.

Sam reciprocated the kiss hungrily and chuckled silently for she knew; M'lyka, her best friend who had introduced her to this man, was probably shaking her head in disapproval. Take it slow Sam! Get to know each other first! You don't know him well enough to... but she did.

Sam may not have known and was in fact not much interested in knowing much about Nelson at the moment, for her body was already aflame and screaming passionately for relief. That at the moment was what mattered to her. Knowing whether Nelson Cheep was anything more than his physical perfection would come later. Sam drove.

It didn't take long to find out more about Nelson Cheep. There were no tears, but suppressed anger and bitterness was enough to make M'lyka stick around most of the time. Her friend wasn't the one to tell you I told you so or I warned you about him, rather, she engaged Sam tactfully in an effort to help her deal with her discovery of Nelson's romp with Jennifer. There'd been a time when she was Samantha's friend and though time had seen her and Nelson drift apart due to differing ideas and ideals concerning relationships, work ethics, and not least his sponging off her the entire time they were together.

"Sam! Sam!" M'lyka's frantic yell brought Samantha back to the present. "Watch out- did you just doze off? You nearly clipped that car!"

"I'm sorry, I just- well, what do you know?" Samantha smiled suddenly.

"You look like you just had a vision," M'lyka's voice still shook from her earlier scare, though it seemed she was fast recovering, "I hope it involves us arriving safely."

"No, I just thought- I have a prospective client to meet!" Samantha quipped suddenly.

"Did you forget?"

"I didn't," Sam smiled, "Just that the client in question was introduced to me by who else?" M'lyka dreaded what was coming for she anticipated it.

"Cheap Nelson!" Sam's nasty gleam was back, "I am meeting with a Mr. Reagan for business purposes!" She shook her fist at the rearview mirror. The silver Dorado was still behind them, "I'll have my revenge Nelson!" she vowed with feeling.

M'lyka could only sigh and worry.

***

Reagan Bold stood and started walking around the table. It hadn't been hard to contact him and using female guiles, set up an appointment with him. The first time they had met, when Nelson had introduced them, Samantha had noticed more than an appraisal of her female form from the man's eyes as well as his tongue, which had kept slithering out of his mouth through moist lips creepily every time their eyes had met.

Samantha drew in a deep breath and readied her mind for what would happen. She had led him on; first with her words when they had first talked over the phone and now, as he seemed to tear off the short, red dress she had worn that morning specifically for this meeting.

He had taken the bait, apparently, but how far was she willing to go just to spite Nelson and perhaps break up a friendship? She didn't want to know, Nelson had hurt her without a second thought. Whatever it took to get back at him.

"What is there to elaborate, Sam?" He crooned and she cringed at the sound of his voice. In her mind she visualized the voice oozing slimily out of a foul mouth to drip in thick and viscous drops... She shuddered suddenly when she felt his hand brush her shoulder.

"We're grownups, aren't we?" Reagan prompted. His hand brushed her shoulder again.

"And?" She prompted him back.

"Aaaand..." He drew the word out as he bent towards her ear. Sam flinched slightly and convincingly, just enough to show him that she was scared, unsure but intrigued and interested. Just as M'lyka had told her. After finding out that Sam had indeed found Reagan and was still intent on carrying out her devious plan as M'lyka called it, she, M'lyka, knowing it was futile to talk Sam out of it had given her pointers on how to carry on with it while maintaining a level of safety. Sam had been afraid of asking her friend where she learned of such dealings with men, since she preferred women.

"...we can decide to please each other." She heard the whispered words slither into her ear, accompanied by a warm breath. *If he tries to force me I'll scream,* Sam thought as she slowly but deftly turned, rose from her seat and faced him. She made sure there was space between them. She observed him through narrowed eyes, though she remembered to retain a Mona Lisa smile; not too much to encourage undesired developments while at the same time just enough to draw a few more words that would explicitly spell out his intentions.

"Having an opportunity to work for you is my pleasure, Mr. Reagan." She stressed on the formality and turned slightly serious, "Unless my portfolio did not impress you."

"It did, your portfolio is impressive enough as it is." He leaned close, then took a slight step forward, "Those offices sure had an expert hand work on their interiors. That's why I'm giving you the job." His smile as he delivered the news resembled a sneer, Sam thought.

"Well then, shouldn't I be starting?" She tugged at her dress while keeping her knees together, gathered up her files and clamping them to her chest, gave him the most professional smile she could muster. Poor man, she had worked him to near stroke and now she was about to leave him hanging.

"Well," Reagan smiled back, though his eyes said otherwise, "This calls for a celebration. Tomorrow night, my place. Don't worry-" he held up a hand when her face reflected objection, "I'll invite everyone if that will make you feel more comfortable. I'll be sure to invite Nelson!"

As she hurried out of the office building and got into her car, Sam wondered what she had started, encouraged to progress and when it had slipped out of her hands. Grabbing her phone, she scrolled through her contacts, wondered who she wanted to call and flung the phone into the next seat. Starting her car, she eased out of the parking lot and drove off into the fast approaching evening.

She drove as if by doing so she would be able to escape everything that was happening, but the faster she drove, the more the thoughts assailed her, and the more she wondered where she had made the first mistake.

Her call was picked up on the first ring.

"M'lyka- I need-"

"My help, I know," M'lyka's voice came through, clear and crisp through the car's radio's Bluetooth connection, "did you give the poor man a heart attack from the way you were dressed?"

"It's nothing like that!" Samantha bit her lip to stifle the expletives that threatened to escape her mouth. M'lyka must have caught the terse note in her voice though.

"Don't bark at me," her voice took on a terseness of its own, "So, did he propose and you're running away?"

"Quit the jokes, M'lyka!" Samantha shouted, "He's invited me to a party tomorrow. At his house!"

"Oh wonders," M'lyka tut-tutted, "it came to that point?"

"He'll invite Nelson too!"

"Wait- didn't you have a plan about getting back at Nelson? Perhaps chance is prostrating itself at your feet. What will you do?"

"First, I'll come by your place-"

"I'm not at home at the moment, so, perhaps a message?"

"Yeah. Please tell me where I can find you so that I may come and strangle you!"

"Aw, Sam is mad. Tell you what, Sam. If Reagan has promised to invite Nelson, then he will, as well as others too. Congratulations on getting the job though."

"Thanks - wait, how did you know that I got the job?"

"Sam, hasn't the foot runner tasked with delivering the message reached you yet? There's social media, and he's posted the invitation! See you there!" The call disconnected with a single beep and a change in screen brightness. Samantha sighed, and sighed again.

She and Nelson were through, at least according to her. Why not just tell him and be done with it? She wondered, and the relief at the simplicity of her idea as well as how easy it seemed it would be in her mind was such that she smiled quietly to herself.

Chapter 2

The night was still young. The party was in full swing, Samantha had been congratulated, Reagan had not done or said anything to further his ulterior motives (yet) she felt, and then, and this was beginning to nag her mind, M'lyka had not yet shown up.

"Miss Binds!" Samantha froze. She had been holding her breath all evening in anticipation, and now it was happening. The 'Miss Binds' thing was especially unsettling, considering how he had salivated and ogled at her the previous day. Composing herself and plastering a party-appropriate- slightly formal but just an enough social smile on her worried face, Samantha turned around.

"Mr. Bold." She made sure to raise her voice slightly, in order to catch the attention of those nearby, in effect saying, he was the last person I spoke to before it happened people. Look into that people! "Thank you for the rare opportunity to work for you-" she stressed the word 'work'.

"I'm pleased to have the opportunity to have your talented hand work this place, Miss Binds, and your tender touch give it the love it deserves." He waved his hand around. His eyes gleamed and Samantha's heart sank.

"The pleasure is all mine, Mr. Bold. Well, I've had a great time-"

"And will continue to," he interrupted her and extended his hand, "Come, I'll show you the very first place I want you to start with."

Feeling that most of the others' eyes were on them, Samantha smiling at him while her smile tortured her facial muscles and Reagan, with a charming smile and an extended hand. Samantha put her hand into his and was whisked away. As she was led away, she caught a glimpse of Nelson.

Their eyes met for a brief moment - before she felt herself ascending a staircase.

"I believe we have unfinished business." The man truly did not waste time. He spoke as he opened a door and held it. Samantha slowed a bit and peeked inside. No bed at least, she thought with relief. She wasn't taking any chances.

"It is my study," he answered her silent query and held open the door wider. Samantha, satisfied that nothing seemed off entered tentatively. He followed. He also left the door wide open. The man was truly no fool.

Samantha, though still wary of doing anything that could trigger unwarranted developments, studied the room. Large, with a high ceiling and oak paneling. High above, a fan spun lazily. A large, Victorian style window faced the east. A mahogany desk on which were numerous files and papers of all colors and sizes was strategically placed such that the morning light would fall on it. Behind the desk was a comfortable looking chair, in which Reagan now sank into with a contented sigh, and placed his glass on the desk. The chair answered by groaning back slightly as his weight settled comfortably into it.

"Let me get straight to the point," Reagan indicated another seat, "I like you, Samantha. If anything has a chance of developing further based on that, I'm all for it."

"Well, Mr. Bold," she pasted on her most formal smile on her face, "we couldn't work together if we hated each other-"

His smile widened, then disappeared at her next words,

"-unless of course you're suggesting anything besides or beyond the job."

"What do *you* think, Sam?" His smile was back, accompanied by a gleam in his eye that she did not like. Suddenly, she decided to end whatever fantasies he was cultivating, though she fully well knew she had perhaps planted and even initially fertilized such ideas.

Feeling emboldened, she stood up and looked at him squarely in the face. His smile disappeared and the gleam faded as if he anticipated what her firmly set mouth was about to utter.

"Listen, Mr. Bold," her eyes did not leave his, "I'm not the kind of woman who jumps into bed with every client as a part of the deal. Nothing is going to happen between us besides the job." She stood up and walked to the door. "Thank you for the party, Mr. Bold."

Sam descended the stairs. Her heart raced and her legs trembled, but her mind was at rest. Suddenly, it dawned on her that she had perhaps lost a huge opportunity to work for the most sought-after client in the state, if not the whole region. *To hell with it*, she thought savagely, *I'm not the first interior designer to lose a job even before it had started.* Putting on a sociable smile, she prepared to mingle with the crowd. The smile was wiped when she notice who was at the bottom of the stairs.

Nelson stood there, drink in hand, foot on the first step, an indecisive or perhaps tortured look on his face.

"I'm thinking of you," were the first words he spoke. Samantha smirked at his words, but when he smiled and she reciprocated, though she failed to feel connected. Neither did his hand placed gently on her hand help.

"Something wrong?" he asked her, a serious look clouding his face. "Didn't we patch things up? Look, I'm ready to..."

"No, nothing is wrong," she answered him evenly. Losing her temper in front of him was the last thing Sam was looking forward to. She had most definitely lost a huge opportunity a moment ago, perhaps tainted her name in the world of interior décor for snubbing a sought-after client, but Samantha wasn't done.

It was time to let Nelson loose too. All of a sudden, it seemed as if all her pent-up frustrations were emboldening her, giving her the courage to assert herself without fear of outcome.

"Sam," Nelson prompted her, "I am really sorry for hurting you. I mean it." Indeed he must have from the way his dark eyes probed into her, just as they had the first time they had met, when he had accused her of hitting an animal. But Samantha was having none of it.

"It is over, Nelson," she said it simply, "I don't need you in my life anymore." With that she left him standing there, perhaps feeling the effects of her words as they sank in. She didn't look back, not even when she heard M'lyka's voice calling her.

I should break my friendship with her too, she thought with a nasty smile as she hurried out of the mansion, into the parking lot, towards her car, and once inside, drove off without letting any thought give her a sense of equilibrium. Before that though, she set her phone to voicemail, *I don't need any calls right now,* she thought.

Once on the road, she whooped into the night with exhilaration. The car must have been in some kind of mood too, for it suddenly joined her by making noises of its own as she drove and yelled into the night. Samantha smiled - and did not stop even when the engine died, just when she was but just a few blocks from home. I'll walk, she decided, nothing can ruin my moment tonight. With that thought held firmly in her mind, she exited the car and started walking.

She didn't stop until she had nearly passed what seemed to be a dog fight, just two blocks away from home. They too weren't going to ruin her night, she decided. Not their snarls or their growls or their whimpers... not even their eerily human-like yells. Human? Perhaps someone was in danger! Suddenly, she stopped and tiptoed towards the direction from which the ruckus seemed to come from. It was a narrow and dimly-lit alley, lined with trash bins and decrepit vehicles. Inside one such vehicle, the dog fight was taking place.

Looking around her, Samantha noticed a brick, or stone, she wasn't sure, but it fitted whatever purpose she had in mind, she decided. Picking it up, she hurled it with all her might. She waited - and heard glass breaking. The fight stopped, but for a moment. Just as the growls and the snarls were resuming, she picked up another brick and hurled it. Her aim was perfect - it landed just as a large snout stuck out of the vehicle, and the brick connected.

Emboldened, she picked up more bricks and started hurling them without stopping. Now the dogs seemed keen on getting out than fighting. They did, rocking the decrepit metal contraption of a car as they exited through the windows. She counted two dogs. Heaving with relief, she turned to leave- when a whimper stopped her. It was coming from inside the car. *Come on!* She thought, *I've done my part!*

With reason and instinct tearing her apart with indecision, she found herself creeping towards the car. She didn't want to find anything in there. She wasn't ready to rescue some injured dog then nurse it back to health. She wasn't ready to invest her feelings in an animal that was perhaps too mauled to survive. But still she crept forward. Blame my morbid curiosity, she chided herself.

The whimpers were gone. There was no motion inside the car. Perhaps those dogs had attacked a homeless person, she thought suddenly and with alarm, and he's dead. Taking out her phone, she switched on its flashlight, and aimed it at the broken window. Just at that moment, a hand grabbed the rusty door and yanked it open.

Tall, she gleaned from the silhouette his frame cast as he struggled to support himself by leaning against the old vehicle. Since the light was behind him, she couldn't make out all of his features clearly. She took a few tentative steps towards him, hands outstretched and ready to defend. As if reading her mind, he moved slightly, and his facial features became slightly clearly discernible. He looked seriously injured.

"Are you okay?" she heard herself whisper in a trembling voice as she fumbled and patted her pockets, "I'm calling for an ambulance." Suddenly she recalled that she had used her phone as a flashlight just before she had run off. I must have dropped it she thought and started looking around and about her.

"Why would dogs attack you?" she asked suddenly as she continued searching, "It hasn't happened for as long as I remember. I don't- hey, you shouldn't stand up! Conserve your energy while I-"

"I'm fine, lady." He had already struggled up. Samantha winced when he felt his face, felt the gash then attempted to wipe of some of the blood with his bare hand.

"Where can I find good food?"

Of all the things she could have expected a stranger who had just been about ripped to shreds to ask or talk about, an opener about food was a new one. Nothing like call someone, nothing like I need to get to a hospital quickly.

Samantha froze momentarily from her search. For someone with such serious injuries, he sounded too calm. And he had an incredibly deep voice.

She didn't know what between the two aspects impressed her more... his asking about food, his calmness, or his deep voice. Perhaps he was yet to understand the gravity of his wounds. Feeling a slight shiver thrill her spine, she picked up a brick. She moved closer, making sure to have the brick in full view. She wasn't taking any chances.

"Mr..."

"Kane, name's Kane." He introduced himself in that same deep voice. Through the dim light, she also noticed that though dusty, he was not filthy. Surely this was no homeless man- he turned slightly and she had a better glimpse of his hair. It was too clean for a homeless person.

"Mr. Kane..."

"Just Kane. Help me sit over there..." Samantha did not move to help, and when he noticed that she didn't intend to, he waved his hand dismissively and crept to where he had indicated, a large, overturned wooden crate on which he sank with a painful sigh.

"Yeah, I'll be okay in a moment." He answered her unasked question. Once seated, he started checking himself methodically, going over every limb from neck, arms, legs and sides. Samantha resumed searching for her phone. She found it and started tapping at its dusty screen- mercifully it had survived her drop and had not cracked.

"Don't call anyone," he surprised her with his curtness, "I'll be fine."

"You're bleeding, Kane. I can't just stand here-"

"Then leave," he seethed suddenly, though there was a hint of pain in his voice. Samantha was taken aback. Surely he hadn't just asked her to leave?

"Excuse me?" she leaned slightly closer. She observed him better just then, for the spot he had chosen had some light from the main street falling onto it. His facial features were more discernible then. He had a nasty gash above his left eyebrow, and his upper lip was torn.

Lowering her eyes to his torso, she felt herself sigh with relief; through what remained of what must have been a shirt, his shoulders, chest and stomach had escaped the canines' teeth. Still he had scrapes here and there, crisscrossing around his midsection. Samantha concluded that his face had borne most of the savagery. Perhaps it had affected his brain too, what with his rudeness.

"Fine, I'm leaving," she pocketed her phone, then after a moment's pause, took it out. "Here," she stretched her hand, "You can call for help when you're done bleeding." He did not move to take the phone. Sighing with what could only have been exasperated wonderment, Samantha placed the phone near his feet, within easy reach. Without looking at him, she started off.

Samantha paused, but did not turn. She still felt irked, though she couldn't have been able to say just why. The stranger's brusqueness was certainly a contributor, not forgetting his nonchalance at her concerns. Indeed, he hadn't thanked her for leaving her phone with him. I have to get it back, he can crawl to the hospital for all I care, she thought as she retraced her steps, back to where he was. He was sitting up straighter, and his brow did not seem to be bleeding much.

Samantha just stared at him sitting there, elbows on his knees, fingers linked, and staring back at her. He seemed stronger than he had been earlier. His dark eyes regarded her silently. Despite his present predicament, he seemed to have about him a kind of dignity, almost regal aura surrounding his person. Or perhaps it was just pride. She decided that a stranger was not going to ruin her already bad night further.

"Well?" he prompted. Samantha noticed that he had not picked up the phone where she had placed it. She leaned over and grabbed it. He did not move. Without a word, she started moving away. She still felt she needed to have a last word though, and once again she found herself retracing her steps.

"Have you forgotten where you were going?" he asked her just as she huffed over, words meant to incinerate that look he had about him already on her lips. The moment his words were out, she stopped still, mouth open.

"What nerve!" she blurted out once she had recovered from the initial shock at his blatant rudeness. She moved closer to him. She was surprised that she was not afraid of him, just mad.

"What is it with you?" she seethed at him as he looked up at her. His dark eyes betrayed nothing, "Why are you being so rude all of a sudden?" She crossed her arms to still her heaving bosom while searing him with her gaze.

"Listen, lady," he stood up with some effort, though he could not stand up straight, "I appreciate whatever you think you've done. Can we part ways without turning this-" he indicated the gap between them with his hand, "-into something else?"

Surely, the man had nerve. She wanted to leave, to be as far away as possible from him, but she still needed to have the last word. She found herself racking her mind's fiery store for a sufficient burn, but seemed to come up with nothing whenever she opened her mouth. *God, when did I turn a saint,* she wondered silently, the words are usually on the tip of my tongue. Suddenly the man chuckled, a deep rumble that reflected in his dark eyes, as if mocking her.

"What?" she bristled. "Shouldn't you be sad?" *Please ask why, please ask why,* she prayed silently-

"Why?"

"The bone you lost to those dogs. No wonder you're hungry. Starve, you deserve it!" With that she turned and huffed off. She did not look back.

Kane still couldn't wrap his head around the fact that for the first time in years, he had danced with death and furthermore, even if he did not want to admit to himself, had been rescued by a human woman. He remained where he was for a while, while thoughts, jumbled up in his mind and jostled for expression.

Topmost among them was the slowly dawning fact that no matter where he hid, he was surely to be found, if they had indeed found him in here. With a heavy sigh, he sank back where he had been sitting and covered his head with his hands. She was close, he knew since he could still sense her scent. He fought off a strong instinct to turn and bound off to hunt, since he understood that he was in a town, though he was yet to know which one it was.

He would know soon enough, he decided, but the town would not know that a werewolf had visited. He stood up and sniffed the air. The woman was still close, perhaps hiding and observing him. Giving it no more thought, he trusted his instincts to lead him into town and to food, good food. Gathering whatever strength he had, Kane stood up and started walking or limping rather.

He exited the narrow alley and found himself on a well-lit street. Few people walked about, and even fewer cars passed. Sniffing the air, Kane walked slowly, while willing himself not to draw any attention.

To his dismay, he discovered that the humans were beginning to more than take an interest in him. Most of his wounds were gone thankfully, but his clothes were dirty and torn. Not much remained of his shirt, and he could feel the breeze between his legs, meaning his pants were torn. He decided to ignore their gawking and move on. He had a purpose and that purpose was to find food. Suddenly, he realized something, and it caused him concern. Using his superior auditory senses, he could hear camera shutters as some people whipped out their phones and started recording him. His worry was not with the humans though.

Technology had dulled most of their inquisitive nature, he knew. Once satisfied with whatever they were recording, they would leave. What worried him was what they recorded, and who would see it once it was broadcasted on what humans called social media.

Instinctive antenna up, Kane retraced his steps and reentered the narrow alley. He would have to find another way of walking around if he was to make any headway. Better clothes or turning, he thought. Since the prospect of clothes seemed remote at the moment, he decided to turn. He lifted up his hands, closed his eyes, and gathering all the strength he could muster, he willed his mind to focus by focalizing his ocular, auditory and olfactory senses; the superior senses of a werewolf. Nothing happened.

Growling at the failure to turn Kane tried again. He drew in deep breaths and willed his mind to focus- but even as he tried, he knew it was futile- his strength was not enough to affect the turning. He would have to heal faster and also regain as much strength as possible. Sighing with exasperation, he started walking out of the alley again- and came face to face with the woman who had- well, she had just interrupted the fight, nothing more.

She stood at the entrance to the alley, looking at him. Kane did not know what she was thinking, but his senses informed him that she was not afraid of him at all. She didn't he was a werewolf, that he was sure, but, why didn't she leave? Why was she still around? Sighing with even more exasperation, he approached- and passed her without a word. Once in the well-lit street, he started walking-

"Are you okay, man?" A young man he was about to pass stopped. "You're bleeding." The young man indicated a cut on Kane's face.

Kane touched his own face and groaned. The effort to turn had reversed some of the healing, for his brow was bleeding again. Snarling with anger and frustration, he headed for the dark alley once again. The woman had not moved. Well, he decided, he would ask her for- just a little help, he decided. She was just a human and couldn't do much for him, but the little she could, he would accept. Decision made, he headed towards her.

Samantha was still where he had left her. She had observed him exit the alley, and now he was headed back. He needs my help, she realized with a thrill, pride won't just let him. Well, here he comes.

She watched him approach and chuckled at his attempt to make himself look as stern as possible. He walked fast though he still limped, the words ready on his lips. As he approached, he held up his hand to put emphasis on what he was about to say- and tripped. Well, there's the pride, and there's the fall, she thought as she hurried towards him- just as he crashed to the ground.

By the time his mind registered that he was falling, he was already on the ground, and someone was leaning over him.

He scrambled up with groans and risked a glance at the woman leaning over him. He realized that this was the first time she was this close to him. Indeed, she was attempting to help him up.

She's laughing, I know it! He thought angrily as he attempted to dust himself off. She was not laughing, though she was looking at him. She was smiling. Feeling mortified, Kane turned and started hurrying off. Where, he didn't know. He was too angry and embarrassed to care. As long as it was somewhere away from the woman who had witnessed his fall, he didn't mind. He heard her call behind him. He did not turn.

Once out of the alley, he checked himself. His trousers were now torn at the knees. His elbow felt odd too, like a cold but burning sensation. He grimaced when he checked; his elbow had a nasty scrape, but it was not bleeding, just that burning sensation.

"You'll need bandages for those scrapes," the voice startled him. He whirled around to see the woman behind him. She fell into step with his limp, her long, dark hair, though pulled back in a ponytail, still blew into her face as she walked beside him.

"I know of a better route if you're to avoid the stares," she spoke again. "And you need clothes I presume?"

Feeling slightly faint as he followed her, he tried to refocus his mind so as to effect a quick healing of his wounds, but it did not work- the woman walking beside him was enough of a distraction. He wasn't afraid of her- even weakened as he was, he still possessed enough strength to overcome any human adversary. She wasn't a danger, he decided. If anything, the woman seemed more intent sticking with him, and through injured pride and pain he had decided to silently accept her invitation, for he was yet to speak to her. Seeing her walking beside him reminded him that he was still hungry.

They had found him. Three of them and he had recognized two of them. Jonah his brother and Luke, his maternal uncle. The third werewolf, the one who had attacked less, Kane didn't recognize. He felt his mind taking him back to how it had come down to this, his own rejecting him and even attempting to kill him, but he was not ready to think about it.

Suddenly, he sensed a difference in and around himself- and realized that the moon was out. It lit the night for a few seconds before dark clouds covered it again, but it was enough to effect changes in Kane. He felt his facial wounds disappearing and he sighed. The woman walking beside him glanced at him sharply. Had she noticed? Did she even know who or what he was? Kane didn't know. What he knew was that his wounds were fast disappearing.

"You're bleeding still," she spoke beside him. "Not too much but enough to require medical attention."

"I'm... I'll be fine," he replied curtly, then added, "As soon as I find a place I can rest." Despite his injuries, his voice was strong, dignified. The pride was still there, she noticed. She bit her lip to stifle the laugh that threatened to escape her, as she recalled his fall.

Just before the thud, she recalled, he had held out his hand as if begging for help. Then he had gone down. And then he had scrambled up and attempted to flee the scene. She had found him and... she glanced at him. He glanced back at her and said nothing. Yep, he had dusted himself, save for his face. His forehead was still bleeding and the tip of his nose was still dusty. Still biting her lip, Samantha stifled a laugh.

If only he wasn't this proud and conceited, she regretted mentally, then I would have helped him further, she thought. As it was, she would point him towards town and then leave him to figure out the rest. Wasn't his need food and clothes?

"Do you have any cash with you?" she asked, then added quickly when she noticed his look. "I mean- to buy food. Surely you don't expect to find a place where they charge pride and arrogance. Did you lose your wallet?" He did not answer.

The moon peeked slightly, and the ma beside her groaned slightly. Sam glanced at him. Surely, hadn't there been a nasty gash above his left eyebrow? She was sure she had seen it, just as he had struggled up after the savage dogs had ran off. He had even had to wipe some of the blood off since it was running into his eye. But now as she observed him in the lunar light, his face had barely any scars.

Sam was not morbid not superstitious, and she thrived in the fact that she did not experience mortal fear. It was something that had been a cause of worry for her overprotective parents since she was young. She suddenly recalled an incident that had happened when she was young, eight or nine. Coming home from school one windy afternoon, a young man had fallen into step with her. She recalled his dark hair and green eyes. He had said nothing, and neither had she. However, she would glance at him, and he would smile. They parted ways when she arrived home. Standing at the gate, she had seen him turn back and return the same way they had come. Once in the house, she had recounted the incident to her mum. Back then she failed to understand why her mum had freaked out so much. The following day, there was a report on the news of a dog that had mauled several people including children, on the same street that Sam used every day, the same street she had used the previous day in the company of a young stranger. Once again, she failed to understand her mum's reaction to the news. Her grandma had insisted that it was her guardian angel who had taken visible form.

But now, as she walked beside the tall man who continued to limp less and less as well as add length to his stride, Sam felt a slight shiver run down her spine. The man beside her was a werewolf. It should have shaken her, but it did not.

So far they had avoided unwarranted attention. Checking her phone, Samantha realized that it was close to midnight. Good thing she had no early morning commitments the following day. She turned to Kane,

"I have food, and a shower. After that you can find a place to spend the night." He did not say anything. Samantha stopped and grabbed his hand. He stopped walking too.

"Listen, Mr. Arrogant," she seethed, "I don't know what your problem is, but when offered hospitality, it is considered good manners to either accept or decline. Politely. Your silent pout does not count."

"How human of you," he said quietly and resumed walking, leaving Samantha standing there. A few steps ahead, he stopped and looked back. Samantha hurried up and when she reached him, he bowed slightly extended his hand. "Lead the way then. I graciously and unpretentiously accept your invitation."

She couldn't tell if he was mocking her or not. His eyes were very serious as he regarded her and waited for a response.

"That works for me," she smiled thinly, "Tag along then, night wolf." Too late she realized that she had let out her discovery. His surprised gasp only confirmed it further, though he said nothing.

Samantha, with sheer effort of will turned all instinctive warnings of her just confirmed suspicions into the prospects that awaited her. It was a thought to relish.

Kane could tell that she wanted, actually itched to talk. He glanced at her as they walked, or she walked and he limped, but less and less. She was a fast walker. Beside her, he matched her quick strides with his by now barely noticeable limp.

It was hotter and more humid than it had been a few minutes earlier.

"It may pour later," she looked up, "Which reminds me, we forgot to talk about the weather."

"The weather, what do you mean?" As if on cue, he shaded his eyes and tilted his head.

"Isn't the weather topic what two strangers talk about?" She looked at him inquisitively. Beads of sweat were mixing up with the dust on his face. In the bright lunar he was a sight, with dried up blood and now sweat mixing with dust.

"I don't know-" he replied. "I find chit chat..." he paused, then shrugged. She spoke before he continued,

"Time wasting, you mean." It was a statement, to which he nodded.

They hurried on.

Now that his pain had receded and his mind had cleared, Kane found himself wondering about the woman he was following. She had invited him, he had accepted. Did she know that he was a werewolf? If she did, why wasn't she afraid? If she did not, would she freak out if she later found out? She had just called him 'night wolf', though she had not revealed more.

Despite his aversion at small talk, he would have loved to talk to her about it. Why she wasn't afraid of him and perhaps what she thought of werewolves in general. He wasn't ready to start the conversation, but one thing he was sure of, she wanted him. He could sense her need with his heightened senses. At first he had chuckled silently at the fact, but now as it became apparent that she was indeed intent, he wondered how it would unfold if she did indeed openly declare her desire for him.

She knew how to tell if one was fit, and listening to him breath as he hurried on beside her, it was evident that he was a man who took his health seriously. He frowned when he noticed her glance at him.

"Just one more street to close further ahead," She announced just as a few drops splashed around them as if to announce that more were to be expected. She hoped the cheerfulness in her voice did not sound forced.

"I'm used to it, the walking," she informed him when she noticed him looking at her questioningly, "You do too, for someone as hurt as you are." Above them the clouds parted slightly, revealing a determined moon. The man drew in deep breaths as if drinking in some kind of power from the moonlight. Sam glanced at him as he walked, hands held in front of him as if welcoming more and more of this unseen power that seemed to regenerate him more and more.

By the time they were crossing an intersection, she was running to catch up with his strong strides. By now used to the moon and clouds' games, they did not notice when darkness fell over once again and this time the drops fell with more force. Just as before, they let up and the air filled with an earthy scent.

Making every effort to dissuade her instincts from feeding her brain with fantasies she did not want to entertain, Sam racked her mind for something else to think about, other than a night with a stranger who would get up in the morning and leave.

He would take with him so much of her and she would be left wondering where she kept going wrong and why she felt so unfulfilled all the time. Wasn't love supposed to fill an innate human need- suddenly a mental image filled her mind. She saw herself kneeling on a very beautiful carpet, looking at young child, who was gurgling happily and looking back at her with such innocent eyes; in her mind it was a boy.

She felt a rush of love as she picked up the boy and walked over to a window, where the two of them looked out. A vehicle had driven up. She saw him get out of the car and wave at them as they looked on. They rushed to the door to welcome him; the child held out his arms to be picked... just as Sam looked at the man she loved, and she found herself wondering why his face was all bloody and dusty.

Suddenly, she realized that Kane had spoken, and her fantasy fizzled away, leaving her to a present reality she was beginning to dread, and hate.

"Um, what?" she turned to him. Her fantasy was gone, but it had left an imprint of that man's face, which was fast beginning to be etched into her memory. Somehow, the stranger walking beside her had walked into her fantasies too. She glanced at him, just as he happened to glance at her too. She didn't mind his getting into her mind as much as getting out; she didn't know if she wanted him to.

"I'm sweating," he mopped his brow, wiping off some of the dust that was turning to grime.

"I am too," she felt pleased at his unprompted rapport, even if it was just a few words. It was more welcome than his earlier rudeness and his lately sullen silence.

"We walk faster then." He added and increased his stride. Sam said nothing but she added to her strides too. By morning, her body would be fulfilled but her mind would be emptier. That is, if the fantasy in her mind became a reality. Up to that moment, Samantha had thought of a night romp, but now she found herself wondering about humans, werewolves and love.

One falling for the other was frowned upon, though it was not a law. As far as she could recall, even from her history, the two communities had kept apart for centuries. They did meet for business or political reasons, but never socially. She realized she was wondering if anything would ever prompt her to fall for a werewolf, and if yes, how would she go about it, knowing the two communities' unspoken rule? Even if the stranger walking beside her fell for her –she rolled her eyes at the thought, then found herself chuckling-what difference would it make? Why was love so elusive, and at times so mercilessly conditional?

Chapter 3

They had arrived. Sam opened the door and once in the hallway, glanced around before beckoning at him. She held her breath as they rode the elevator to the third floor though they met no one. She did not relax until they were safely inside her apartment. Indicating that he remain standing where he was, Sam did a slow, methodical appraisal, disregarding his discomfort at being gawked at that way.

He was tall, muscular with sinewy muscles bunching out of every tear of what must have been a shirt and he had dark hair. For the first time, Sam noticed that he wore it rather long, and some of it covered his face. His eyes were very dark and he had very thick eyebrows, though it was hard to tell due to the grime that covered his face. The man was truly dirty.

"I'll- what do you prefer? A bath or a shower?" she asked him.

"A cold river," he answered back. Not able to tell whether he was attempting humor, Sam shrugged and left the room. Presently and before he could move, she was back.

"Take off what remains of your clothes," she ordered him. "Shower it is." He hesitated then started tearing what remained on his grimy body. When it came to his torn pants, he glanced at her. She did not flinch.

"Well?" he prompted.

"Well what?" she challenged him.

"Do you want me to undress in front of you?"

"Is it a problem?"

"It- well, ah... I've never been in this situation before..."

"Don't tell me no woman has ever seen you naked." Still he made no move to undress further. Sam crossed the room and stood in front of him. His reluctance to undress in front of her was strangely turning her on. Standing very close, she looked up at him. His dark eyes seemed to reflect a conflict within.

"What if I want to be here when you undress?" she crooned softly.

"What if I don't want to?" he asked quietly.

"What if I made you want to?" she stood even closer.

"What if I did something that made you not want to?" he asked in such a deep voice, it sounded like a growl.

"What if what you did made me want to even more?" she could no longer hide her desire for him.

"What if I didn't feel the same way?" she could tell from the dark gleam in his eyes that she had aroused his instinctive need, but a conflict within was keeping it in check.

"Are you sure?" he growled again, "Lady, do you know what you are asking for?"

"What if we stopped asking each other such questions?" she took a step back and devoured him with her eyes. Suddenly, she stepped aside and pointed, "Small hallway to your left, second door. Call if you need anything." With a grateful nod, he crossed the room and disappeared to the left.

Presently, she heard the shower running. Sam felt her stomach drop, and with it, all the giddy feelings floated away, leaving her with a loud gasp and an emptiness that made her want to cry. Had she been scorned? She hated the word. Had that man turned down her advances? Should she throw him out? The shower continued running while such thoughts raced in her mind.

Kane had never been a fan of hot water. Ever since he could recall from a young age, he preferred cold, icy water running down his body, never mind the time of day, to hot, steaming water. As he stood inside the bathroom and familiarized himself with everything, his mind took him back to what had just happened earlier. Not the attack, he wasn't yet ready to think or even ruminate about that, but what had happened between him and the woman, Samantha Binds. She had been very direct. Kane liked assertive women, who knew what they wanted and did what they had to get it. Back in Hale it had been a problem to find a mate with such attributes, since a majority of his kind still stuck to the old ways of dominance and submission.

His last female companion had left him due to this very reason- his aversion to olden mores, terming them archaic and petrified in time. Now, the woman who's brought me here, he thought as he started the shower and stood under the cold water, the woman is something else. She has guts, he thought.

Sam picked up the tatters that had been his shirt and walked with them over to the trash bin. She swung her hand to throw it in, then paused as a thought suddenly struck her- where was he going to get new clothes? It was night, and it was late. Nelson, her ex had left a few items of clothing, and she had stuffed them somewhere during one of her anger-fueled general cleaning of the apartment. She wasn't about to go digging them out to help someone who didn't seem to understand what she wanted.

She'd have taken her car, rushed to town and got him something, but his rebuff at her advances earlier had left her in a bad mood. She wasn't about to do him any favors. If he needed to be dressed, then he would have to go to town himself.

With such resolve in mind, Sam walked into the kitchen with the aim of fixing herself a cup of cocoa. Task accomplished, she walked back to the living room, steaming cup in hand. Just at that moment, he appeared, dripping wet, dark hair stuck covering his eyes, and a tiny towel tied around his waist. He paused when he noticed her, then took a step back when his eyes fell on the steaming cup in her hand. She must have noticed it or perhaps not, but she place the cup on a nearby shelf and unsure of what to say, stepped tentatively towards him.

"Um, thank you for the shower," he spoke first, "It was very refreshing."

"You're welcome?" she shrugged and linked her hands together, "I'm sorry I was a bit too much earlier. I was coming from a party and must have had too much..."

"Don't apologize. I blame myself if I contributed too," he held up a hand, "But I'm fine."

"But you have nothing to wear," she heard herself say, "Are you okay with just a towel?"

"No."

"Well, I..."

"I'm not taking it off in front of you." He added suddenly.

"I'm not asking you to. I just wanted to tell you I have a few items of clothing which belonged- well, I have a few you could borrow."

"Well?" he prompted her.

"Well what?"

"Could you get me a shirt and pants?"

"I said you could borrow not demand!"

"Well then," he stepped closer, "Please, may I borrow a shirt, pants, and perhaps inner wear from you? All male habiliments if you please."

Samantha stifled a laugh, but mostly because she could not tell whether he was joking or not. Certainly, his eyes were darkly serious as he regarded her and waited for a response.

"Sure, why not. Follow me."

***

"Where will you stay then?" She asked bluntly.

"That shouldn't bother you," he replied curtly without looking at her. Clean and well dressed- fortunately, he and Nelson seemed to have the same height, for the clothes fitted, though Kane was more muscular, and his muscles showed more through the blue shirt and white trouser pants that she had picked out for him. Once dressed, he had headed for the door.

"Thank you." He said it simply, without much feeling.

"Welcome," Sam replied with emotion. "Where are you going?"

"Out. I'm cleaned, thank you, I have clothes, thank you. Now I will go- I needn't ask for anything else."

Samantha stood up and placing her steaming cocoa on the table, approached him. He did not move when she stood so close, she could see his heartbeat through the tight shirt.

"You were hungry, remember?" she asked him, "And I have food. In any case it is raining. Sit, I have- what do you eat?"

"What do you mean?" He did not move away from the door. Samantha, who had started to walk towards the kitchen, noticed that he was still standing there and paused.

"Well, I have no raw meat- and as arrogant as you have been so far, I wouldn't suggest dog food..." suddenly he bounded across the room towards her.

"What do you know?" he snarled at her. Samantha, unfazed, looked into his dark eyes, then did what she had been itching to do- well at least part of it- she placed a hand on his wide, hard chest. They remained like that for a moment. It was one of those rare but memorable moments which Time obeys and they become timeless.

Slowly slid her hand across his chest and acknowledged her thrill at his quickening heartbeat with a sudden intake of breath. Emboldened by his favorable response, Samantha reached out with her other hand and finding his, she pulled it around her waist. He did not resist. She pressed herself even closer and willed him to hold her tighter, which he did to her effusive thrill. She couldn't stop staring at those lips, inching closer... closer... just as his other hand reached up and took hold of hers which was still on his heaving chest. He grasped it, and right at that moment, Kane felt that much than could have been said with words was effectively passed between them through their locked eyes, close bodies, and their linked hands.

This was a woman that he didn't know, someone he had met not more than an hour earlier. But as they stood there silently communicating, he had that strange and unexplainable conscious realization that he and she were somehow connected, that whatever was happening between them at the moment was very right and meant to be. This is what perfection means, he thought, just as his mind, unable to fully get hold of and express that strange conscious realization, let go of it and returned to default; in which he realized that he was holding a woman's hand, a woman he barely knew, and a human at that. He let go of her suddenly and moved away. She remained where she was while none said anything to the other.

Contrary to the earlier silence when Time had created for them a moment, the silence this time was painfully loud and each felt that they had to say something.

"I'm not the type. Sorry." He did not look at her. She did not reply nor do anything to indicate that his words had had any effect on her. Silently, she picked up her now warm cocoa and walked to the kitchen. Kane was left to wonder if he should leave, sit or continue standing. Before he could do anything, she was back.

"I have beef, and it is cooked," she said it simply then disappeared back into the kitchen. Well, that means sit, he decided and sank into the nearest seat. In a moment, delicious smells wafting from the kitchen reminded him of how hungry he was. His stomach answered the smells with a grumble, and Kane settled to wait.

The meal was a simple affair, shared silently. As Kane dug into his beef gyro, his mind brought him to the realization that so far, the woman sitting opposite him had done so much. He appreciated all her efforts, but he couldn't bring himself to express it with words.

As such, it remained that if he attempted to leave immediately after the meal, she would be highly offended as humans were highly emotional beings. If he lingered any longer though- well, it was a prospect he still wasn't willing to explore, but as the tasty meal settled in his stomach, his senses, now freed of their task of reminding him of hunger, turned to the next significant thing. Body relief.

Despite his desperate situation, he felt a hot rush of warmth spread all over his chest and a slight throbbing in his groin as he regarded her sitting there eating quietly. So far she had said enough to let him know that he was a werewolf, she had more than indicated her interest in him, so what held him back? Suddenly, he realized it with a gasp. Humans had a complicated definition of lust, infatuation, love and commitment. To humans it was possible to detach the physical act from all emotional connections. Not so with werewolves.

Sex and love were intricately woven together, though to Kane, what they defined as love was more of a sense of duty. To humans, love held an entirely different connotation. To yield himself to her, he needed to feel, he needed to connect more than physically. Unfortunately, if what she was after was mere physical release, then he would be left in a quandary. Still, would it hurt to know her better if indeed it was bound to happen?

Compared to what he was running away from, would sleeping with her leave him any much worse than he was at the moment? Kane had never experienced the feeling that engulfed him at that moment as he sat there sharing a meal with a woman he had just met earlier; he had always felt in control, ahead of every situation, good or bad, but most of all, Kane Limaric had never imagined himself at the mercy of another person. Now, he felt helpless.

"What do you know about me?" he asked suddenly. She did not respond immediately, but regarded him silently for a moment. Then, replacing her fork, she leaned closer as if she intended to whisper the answer. Instinctively, he leaned towards her.

"You are a werewolf," she revealed, "Who is afraid of women. Human women." She whispered the last words slowly. "Kane," she challenged him with her eyes, "You. Are.

Afraid. Of. Human. Women." It took but a moment. With a snarl, he knocked over the small dinner table as he lunged. She had been waiting. When he lunged, she was already on him, and the blue shirt was already torn.

Their lips clashed. She attacked him with a hunger that surprised him, but he did not have a moment to dwell on it. He felt her impatient tongue probing, thrusting, yearning, wanting. He responded, and as he felt her respond in kind, his mind jumped into the fray too, convincing him that this was their first and last moment together.

He stood to lose something valuable if he did not take the chance there and then by making the most of it. Feeling giddy with renewed pleasure, he found himself deepening the kiss. He groaned, and held her even closer. She responded in kind, by wrapping her arms around his waist and taunting his aching groin by rubbing against him slowly. Lips meshed, they silently continued finding a part of each other they couldn't have found otherwise.

In truth their bodies were not so quiet; they screamed with yearning, they melted with inflamed passions and as they melded into each other, they found a uniting voice which could not have been expressed otherwise.

Suddenly, he extricated himself and stepped away from her. When Samantha jumped up, he held his hand to indicate that she stay away. He kept his face hidden away from her.

"What is it, Kane?" She asked with alarm, "Did I hurt you - are you bleeding again?" Suddenly, the prospect seemed very real. She touched her face - nothing. The floor, nothing. What was wrong with him then?

"Don't come closer!" he warned her suddenly when she started to approach him. "Just give me a moment!"

Samantha was confused. What could have - suddenly, she observed him, turned away from her as he was. Slowly, it dawned on her what could have happened.

"Kane," she called him kindly, "I understand- you started turning, is that it? You couldn't control it- are you afraid that I might be scared?" She waited and saw him nod slowly.

He still had his back turned away from her, and his face in his hands. She approached him slowly, tentatively. She felt that he was more afraid than she was, for as she stretched out her hand and placed it gently on his back, she felt him flinch slightly.

"Kane, I'm not afraid. Kane, look - just look at me? Please?"

"You'll scream," he spoke through his hands, "And they'll come. They will pour hot water all over me..." What was he talking about, she wondered?

"Kane, I promise. I am not afraid. Look, I knew what you were even before you had told me. Did I show any fear-?"

"Stay away!" he warned her suddenly and headed towards the door, "I need to be as far away as possible." With that he flung open the door and fled. Samantha was left there wondering what had just happened.

In a moment he was back. He no longer covered his face, which Samantha, despite her relief at his coming back and confused anger at his earlier conduct, took a moment to observe. Nothing looked out of the ordinary. When he noticed her looking at him, he attempted a placatory smile. That is when she noticed the fangs.

"Oh God." She heard herself whisper.

"I'll leave-you don't have to be alarmed or anything-" he turned towards the door, but she lunged at it and positioned herself between it and him.

"You're not leaving until you tell me what has just happened."

"I started turning. You said it. Now, may I leave?" she did not budge, but shook her head vigorously, "It was more than that. What was that about hot water?" At the mention of hot water, he snarled suddenly, then drew in deep breaths as if trying to control whatever had suddenly possessed him. His canines had receded considerably, though his eyes still had a dark glimmer as he regarded the woman standing between him and whatever waited out there. Sensing that she had no fear whatsoever, he relaxed and walked over to the seat. He sank into it and did not resist when she came and joined him by sitting next to him and taking his hand. None spoke. Outside, the rain continued battering the windows.

When she opened her eyes, she looked around her. She was in her bed, but she couldn't remember getting into it. Suddenly everything came rushing into her mind and she jumped out of bed. She rushed into the living room and - she sighed with relief when she noticed the form hunched on the couch, legs hanging over one armrest.

Tiptoeing closer, she noticed that he was deeply asleep. His breathing was deep and regular. She went back into her bedroom and presently returned with a blanket, which she covered him with. She walked over to the window and peered outside. The sun was already up and had already warmed a wet world, she noticed.

With another glance at the sleeping form, she started clearing by picking up the dining table and collecting the scattered plates. She glanced at him again. He had not stirred. Walking into the kitchen, she started her morning routine. She did not hear anyone enter the kitchen.

"Who is the stud?" M'lyka's voice whispered beside her. Samantha whirled around, a scream on her lips. It took a moment to gather her mind as she set down the pan she had raised in defense. M'lyka laughed.

"What is gotten into you?" she asked her friend, "You're shaking all over! First time I've seen you this terrified!"

"Did you have to creep in like that?" Samantha asked sternly. The sudden adrenaline rush had left her feeling weak and wobbly. She sank into a chair and regarded her friend angrily.

"Well, I called, you wouldn't answer. I knocked you wouldn't open the door. I let myself in, worried sick after the events of last night-"

"Events? What events?" Samantha asked suddenly. She recalled Kane, torn and bleeding limping beside her and gawkers taking pictures. Had M'lyka found out? Suddenly, she realized that they couldn't talk there. That was a werewolf asleep on her couch. If awake, he would catch every word between the two, and then he would flee. Samantha did not want to think about it. He could leave if he wanted to of course- he wasn't a prisoner in her apartment, but she wanted him to want to return.

She stood up and pointed, "In there," she pointed towards the bedroom, "Follow me." M'lyka obeyed.

"Shhh!" Samantha shushed her when she opened her mouth to speak, "Give me a moment to change. Don't peek, can't you see he's sleeping?" she rebuked her friend with a hoarse whisper when M'lyka craned her neck to better see the sleeping form. Samantha pulled her to the bedroom and did not allow her to speak until she had closed the door. Even then, she whispered.

"We can't talk here," Samantha whispered as she changed. M'lyka could only give her friend a quizzical frown and nod.

"I have a mind to pound you to dust!" M'lyka let it out once they were out of the apartment and on the road. Her place wasn't that far, but Samantha wasn't willing to walk. They took her car.

"Is that how you greet your best friend?" Samantha grinned at her friend. "Wipe that scowl off your face and smile back!"

"Why should I? You ran off last night, and you switched off your phone! I come into your apartment, and what do you know?"

"Cool down, M'lyka," Samantha gave her friend a placatory smile, "We'll talk about it, but not at the moment."

"When? And why was he on your couch? In Nelson's clothes? Is he a visiting relative, one I never knew you had?"

"Yes, my long lost brother..."

"Please," M'lyka rolled her eyes. They had arrived at her place.

"What is with that, Sam? I was worried sick! Are you that heartless- what happened by the way?"

She was onto her friend the moment they were inside. M'lyka was the very opposite of Samantha when it came to organization. Her house was one mess of paint cans, canvases, wooden frames and in one corner, electric tools of various shapes and designs.

Samantha tiptoed around paint cans, brushes, and other artist's paraphernalia as she wiggled herself around paintings, most of them half done. She could feel M'lyka's searing look a she settled herself on a misshapen couch.

"I may have lost a lucrative opening with Reagan." She announced once she was uncomfortably settled on the couch, though it was more of in the couch from how deep it was. "Why do you keep this thing?" she pounded it with her fist, "It will ruin your back..."

"And?" M'lyka prompted, "Lucrative opening-Reagan-"

"Well, that's done." Samantha replied simply.

"What did you tell him?"

"That I didn't find him attractive enough..."

"What?" M'lyka's eyes widened in disbelief.

"Not in so many words," Samantha lifted a hand, "Just enough."

"How did he take it?"

"I don't know, didn't give him a chance to respond," Samantha shifted uncomfortably. "Can we talk about something else? Please?"

"What did you say to Nelson?"

"I ended it."

"And?" M'lyka prompted again.

"And nothing. I did not give him a chance to respond."

"Well," M'lyka stood up, knocking over her easel as she did, "Shit!" she cursed quietly, then crossed over to the counter. She started selecting paint tubes, opening them and sniffing their contents. Her voice changed with every sniff, as one slight cough morphed into a coughing fit. The tube contents were affecting her, it seemed. Samantha waited- "He did respond, as did Reagan. You set off a fire, Sam." She managed to blurt amidst a cough. "You did it."

"What?" Samantha felt her heart begin to hammer. "What did they do?" M'lyka did not answer immediately. Walking back to her stool, she picked up the fallen easel and started setting it up again. She also picked up the stretched canvas she had placed on it earlier and after inspecting it for damage and finding none, repositioned it on the easel.

"Well?" It was Samantha's turn to prompt her friend. M'lyka started painting.

"The two men fought, Sam. In front of everyone, and the reason was you."

Chapter 4

When he woke up Kane found himself alone in a quiet house. Must have gone to work, he thought. He felt claustrophobic, and he was ravenously hungry. Time to go out and- well, perhaps get to know the town he had nearly died in. On the table in front of him were folded bills. He picked them up and after counting them, selected a few notes and put the rest back on the table.

He checked himself- the shirt she had given him hours earlier was torn. He walked into her bedroom and feeling like an intruder, he opened the closet where she had pulled out the shirt from earlier. He pulled out a black shirt. Walking to the bathroom, he stripped and showered, then dusted and wiped his shoes.

Afterwards, he cleaned after himself and dressed. Should I write a note? He wondered. He walked back into the living room and noticed a small desk in the corner- had it been there- on which was a notebook and pens.

Went to the park

He placed the note next to the bills and walked out. It didn't take long to reach town and to find a restaurant.

Despite his hunger, Kane took a moment to admire the inside of the place. A quick glance of the general interior layout was enough to tell him that it was a casual place, with none of the defining formal features that he had been accustomed to in Hale. All the same, he appreciated that it was not fast food.

The dining area reminded him of a religious abode; seats and tables on the right and left side much like pews, a wide throughway leading to the counter at the front, just as an altar would be. He decided that the seats and tables were well arranged; not too squeezed together, and at the same time not too spaced out, just enough for waiters to weave through. The walls on the left and right of the entrance were very interesting. As well as images of the various foods offered, they were adorned with pictures of growing plants with ripe fruit.

The front of the building had large windows that let in natural light, giving the whole place a quiet, homely atmosphere. Perhaps not what I would have expected in a human town, he thought. No fancy chandeliers, glaring lights or live music, as the stereotypes went, just a quiet ambience that he welcomed with all his being, at least for the moment. Perhaps it was the hunger making him admire a place he wouldn't have otherwise bothered with had he been in his element, he wasn't sure.

One thing he was sure of though, the place had food. Good, he wasn't sure, but Kane didn't care. Now that he was here and still hungry, he started searching for the best place to sit. The place didn't seem busy at the moment, though one or two uniformed busboys could be seen wiping the tables and rearranging the chairs. When a menu was placed in front of him, he didn't hesitate. He wanted the dish that reminded him of her, and that is what he ordered.

He was still deep in thought when a waiter placed a tray in front of him. On it was beef and gyro stew, the same he had enjoyed earlier. With a grateful smile and heartfelt thanks, he dug right in.

"Now to your brother," M'lyka dipped her brush and touched the canvas with it, "What is the story?"

Samantha just shrugged, then stood up.

"I'm hungry," she announced suddenly. M'lyka regarded her for a moment, then pointed, "Check the kitchen." Samantha headed to where she had been directed, glad to leave M'lyka for a moment. Her friend's voice followed her though as she stepped around cans, "Careful! Don't spill the paint in your hurry to run away!"

Samantha smiled to herself. Nothing, it seemed, escaped her friend. She heated some pasta and sat at the kitchen table to enjoy it-

"What have you found out about him?" M'lyka asked loudly, and Samantha jumped, spilling the pasta on herself. Her friend was leaning against the door, rubbing paint off her fingers.

"Crap!" Samantha cursed then turned to her friend, "What is it with you and creeping around- did you just follow me?" she asked lividly.

"Well, I'm waiting for the paint to set." M'lyka replied calmly. "While I wait, perhaps you can tell me more."

"About what?" Samantha stood up and served herself another plateful.

"That man in your apartment, on your couch. Your long-lost brother!"

"Well, he's just that, satisfied?" Samantha took a bite of her pasta and did not look at her friend.

"No."

"What do you want?" Samantha indicated with her fork. "Your paint has set, go finish the piece." M'lyka smiled and walked into the kitchen. She poured herself a cup of coffee and sat. Samantha glared at her.

"Now, don't give me that look, Sam. Other than that he's muddled your brain in some way, what else don't I know?"

"Should I figure it out?"

"Not much to figure," Samantha smiled slightly, "but knock yourself out."

"A stranger for a one night revenge sex- but then, he would have been on your bed, not folded on the couch. Perhaps you met, romped, but he crossed a path- but then you wouldn't have left him money... and the fact that he was wearing Nelson's clothes... indeed a mystery, indeed and truly a mystery." Samantha said nothing.

She stood up and started fixing herself a cup of cocoa. From the uncomfortable silence, it was obvious that M'lyka was waiting for her to speak.

"I found him, naked and hungry, took him home, cleaned him, fed him and gave him a place to spend the few hours remaining till morning." She glanced at her friend, "And that is the truth."

"Oh Sam," M'lyka's smile resembled that of a moral teacher correcting a wayward pupil. "If only it was that easy."

"What? I just spilled it all. You've practically cajoled it out of me."

"Well, unless there is something very unique or special about him- Why would a man be out and naked on a rainy night? Is he running away from something?"

Sam feigned ignorance at her friend's sleuthing. Sometimes M'lyka could be nosey. Samantha felt the familiar irritation welling up from deep within. It took two deep breaths to contain herself, for she could feel the nasty words she yearned to blurt out forming in her head.

"He's not a criminal, if anything, he- well, I'd be dead already, wouldn't I?" Samantha hoped she sounded better than she heard those words echo in her head. She knew it was a lame attempt; trying to defend someone she had just met, someone who reeked of mysteries, secrets and a unique fear of humans.

Still, part of why she felt she had to help him was that she felt she owed it to herself to unlock his fears; she could have left him at any moment once she was sure his perceived danger was over, but she had spent her time with him.

She didn't want to dwell on their kiss too much though, for fear of overthinking about it, as well as what had followed after. Unusual it had been, but worthwhile, and certainly to be yearned for again. It was on this premise that Samantha put out his case so passionately.

"Did he tell you that? Did he also say that it was all a mistake, that he didn't do it?" M'lyka's voice broke the silence.

"What are you talking about?"

"That's what all criminals say Sam- escaped convicts, psychos say! They're also very good kissers!"

"M! Please- I trust my instincts, and you trust me in turn!"

"What if something happens? I'm being serious now Sam- what if- I don't know, he strangles you in your sleep?"

Samantha stood up and walked to the sink.

"Well?" M'lyka persisted. "I found a stranger in your apartment," she persisted- "And I'm yet to understand why he was sleeping on your couch and not-"

"I'm not sure I know what you're talking about," Sam cut her friend off as she busied herself with cleaning the few dishes that were there. After what had happened with Nelson a few months back, she wasn't willing to let her mind dwell too much on topics of men and relationships or even love-making. Not even to M'lyka, her best friend. She sighed as she banged a few cups around, opened the cabinet then closed it savagely, filled the sink, emptied it, filled it again... but M'lyka was a patient girl, a trait that Sam resented at the moment. Why did her best friend seem to be on her case this much, she wondered as, after having rearranged and banged several things around, she finally sunk into a chair and sighed loudly. M'lyka smiled.

"You done?" she asked sweetly, but to Sam it seemed as if her voice and words mocked her. There was no escape, she could only come clean.

"If I tell you will you ease off?"

"Sure." M'lyka smiled, but to Sam who glanced at her with annoyance, it looked more like a wicked grin, one that needed to be knocked off with a fist. It would be accompanied by a few teeth too.

"Who is he?" M'lyka asked with renewed interest.

"Kane is a-"

Just then, M'lyka's phone trilled loudly. She suffered a moment of indecisiveness, then stood up suddenly.

"Kane is his name- hold it right there, Sam. That could be the call I've been waiting for all week."

Samantha sighed with relief. Would it have been wise to reveal Kane's identity, even if it was to her best friend? She listened to M'lyka quoting figures on her phone, and just then an inspiration hit her. Standing up, she found her friend and mimed that she had to leave. She couldn't resist a guffaw at M'lyka's stern look, since she couldn't cut short her call.

With a final wave, Samantha tripped over cans of paint, pieces of wood and made her escape. She let out the laughter once she was outside. Glancing back, she glimpsed her friend peering at her through the window, and shaking her fist at Samantha, phone still held to her ear.

"I swear, one of these days I'm going to really pound you into dust. Grind you up and then watch with satisfaction as the wind blew you away!"

"Oh, hello, M!" Come in please!" Samantha bade her friend. After leaving her M'lyka's place and finding Kane gone but having left a note, Samantha had resumed her cleaning. However, she knew that M'lyka was not far behind. She had been right. Barely half an hour later, M'lyka was at her doorstep, fuming and threatening fire and hailstorm.

"That was quick," Samantha observed glibly. "Car?"

"I walked!" M'lyka sank into a chair and mopped her brow, "Get this, Sam, the shiftier you behave, the more your night guest quips my interest."

"Where is he?" she whispered suddenly while looking around her.

"He's gone," Samantha answered her, "Satisfied?"

"Not really. Who is he?"

"I told you, you wouldn't believe me. But would you believe it if I told you I was still hungry?"

"Well, that I would believe. You are a voracious eater, Sam. But we're not changing the subject!" She shouted to a retreating Sam who disappeared in the kitchen. Presently, she reappeared, a bowl of fruit and salad in hand. She settled comfortably at the dining table and started devouring the contents of the bowl. M'lyka just stared at her.

"What?" she asked through a mouthful. M'lyka just shook her head when suddenly; something seemed to catch her immediate attention. She stood up and crossed over to the living room table. When Samantha turned to see what had held her friend's interest she gasped and nearly chocked on a piece of melon.

"A note?" M'lyka held it as if it contained incriminating evidence. "Went to the park," she read. "What does that mean? He'll be back." She dropped the note back on the table and sashayed back to where Samantha sat. Her bowl was already half empty.

"You know what?" M'lyka sat and leaned closer. Sam made the effort to do the same, though she could sense the dread begin to well up in the deep of her stomach at the conspiratorial tone her friend had taken. She waited. M'lyka's eyes gleamed. "There are rumors in town..."

"What rumors?" Sam heard herself blurt out. She dreaded the answer she was waiting for, as if she already knew what her friend was about to say.

"Prevatya Sartram was in town last week..."

Samantha gasped. Prevatya Sartram was a representative of the Council of Ethics in Hale. His presence in a human city could have meant only one thing, and M'lyka's next words, hushed and meant to shock from the way she delivered them, drew another gasp from Samantha.

"They have a rogue over there. A werewolf escaped justice and may be hiding here in Green Bay!"

"Surely they must have evidence that he is here." Sam heard herself whimper faintly. Her heart was beating very fast.

"He?" M'lyka lifted her eyebrows, then smiled knowingly. A twinkle Samantha did not like for one beat played in her dark eyes. "It is a she from what I heard."

"What?" Sam blurted and nearly choked. She didn't know whether to feel relieved or even more alarmed; relieved that M'lyka wasn't talking about Kane, or alarmed at the thought of a she-wolf after her mate. Kane had not divulged much all this time. Was there more to it than he was letting on? Was he burying it all and covering it with his arrogance, sometimes punctuated by bursts of chivalry? As these questions ran through her mind, she felt the panic begin to rise. M'lyka was still talking.

"I'm thinking of looking for her." She winked. "You know, find out."

"Find out what?" Sam felt the dread rising in her once again. She anticipated M'lyka's next words with bated breath.

"Just one night in bed with her." She winked again. "Find out if the rumors are true." Samantha could only shrug.

"I wonder what it is like to be with one, you know?" She placed her elbow on the table and held her cheek in her open palm.

"I- well, you'd have to find out, I think."

"Wouldn't it cause problems?" M'lyka's smile was not that pleasing to Samantha, "Rules and all?"

"It isn't a law as far as I know," Samantha took a tiny bite of pineapple and chewed. She had lost taste in the salad.

"It isn't," M'lyka's grin widened, "But who better to tell it than someone who has met a werewolf and probably made love with them?"

Sam's appetite fled, leaving her with a sour taste in her mouth. Looking at her bowl, she wondered why she had found the cold mush of various fruits appealing.

M'lyka and her veiled insinuations! At least that is what Samantha considered them to be, outrageous claims. She brushed aside the nagging and persistent thought in her mind about Kane and their escapade, shoving them in the darkest recesses of her consciousness. If M'lyka went ahead with her wild plan- and Sam knew she would- then all hell would break loose.

***

As the day progressed and with no sign of Kane, Samantha felt the panic rise. In her mind, she saw him apprehended, and after endless questioning, revealing how he had come her. Nelson's clothes would be paraded as evidence. Numerous video clips as well as photos of the two of them, taken as they had walked to her apartment... and then, they would come for her. Shaking violently at the imagery, Samantha grabbed her phone and jumped in alarm- there was a knock at the door. Drawing in a deep breath, Samantha crossed over and opened it tentatively.

"Kane-" she was shaking. Her earlier thoughts, coupled with M'lyka's words and now the sudden relief at seeing him standing there at her door in Nelson's black shirt was all too much for Samantha. Feeling the emotions overcome her, she burst into tears as she crashed into him. He held her and half-supporting half pushing her inside, he closed the door.

Once inside, Samantha sought solace in his strong embrace as they stood in the middle of the room, while giving vent to her pent-up emotions. It didn't take long. In a minute, she was done, though she was still heaving.

"I'm so sorry, I don't know what came over me," she sniffed, then looked up at him. "You must be shocked at my conduct."

"I sensed distress when you opened the door. Did you receive some bad news?"

"Well, in a way- but I'm not sure. Only you can clear up things Kane." She felt him tense and looked up at him. "Will you? If not everything, then at least a bit?" She thought he wouldn't answer, but then he nodded slowly without looking at her. She observed him a moment further as questions filled her mind and yearned for answers, though she felt she wasn't ready to get all of them at the moment. One thing she had to deal with though, before things went too far. She cleared her throat, "Am I in danger Kane? Are we humans in danger?"

"I don't think so... I'll have to apologize, but I'm yet to learn your name."

"Seriously?" All this time we've been together..."

"It's just been a few hours, and I told you mine the moment we met."

Samantha sensed mild rebuke in his statement, but she did not wish it to sully things. They had been progressing well up to that moment.

"Samantha Binds," she introduced herself, then laughed. "It feels silly, realizing you've been calling me 'lady' all this time."

"Kane Limaric," he bowed slightly. Samantha thought he was jesting, but he had a serious look on his face. "I waited for you to correct me by providing your legal name, but you delayed, hence the 'lady'," he explained.

Suddenly, feeling overwhelmed at the light moment they had just shared, Samantha took his hand, but still unable to contain herself, embraced him tightly. He took a moment before she felt his hands wrap around her waist.

"Not on my watch." He murmured in her ear. "You are not in danger on my watch."

"Is that a promise or are you just saying it to make me feel safe?" she murmured back.

"I don't make promises." He rumbled firmly, "I keep them." They remained as they were for a moment, but it had to end. He released her and walked over to the couch. He sank into it and leaning forward, placed his elbows on his knees and linked his hands. Looking up at her as she stood there looking down at him, Samantha could only sigh.

With what, she didn't but one thing she was sure of, rogue or no rogue, Kane Limaric was a werewolf she was willing bet her chances on. Of all that they had been through so far, his reluctance at her advances stood out the most; it only made her ache for him more and more.

She closed the gap between them and stood over him. She knew that he could tell of her hunger for him. His body was slowly responding to her closeness from his rapid breathing and tauntingly inviting lips, though she could detect an inner conflict in his mind, reflected through his dark eyes. She held her ground though, her own heart raced too, and her lips yearned to meet his.

Making an effort not to look away from his piercing gaze, she waited. She wanted him to make the move.

He did. Feeling overwhelmed with a very strong urge to hold her closer, he yearned to reassure her that it would be alright, that he would be safe and there for her always. She was standing very close to him till he could feel her warm breath. Without waiting for his mind to decide for his body, Kane took her hand, pulled her even closer and kissed her.

Samantha heard herself gasp when he pulled away and gazed into her eyes.

"You have to be patient," he articulated each word slowly, as if to let each sink. "If you really mean this. If you want it."

"How do I do that, Kane? Where do I find the patience when my desire for you scorches without mercy?" He gazed at her a while longer, then his face lit up,

"Come." He stood up and held out his hand. "Let's go for a walk. But first, may I borrow a sweater perhaps?"

Samantha, with a quick nod disappeared into the bedroom, then reappeared with a hooded cardigan. Kane took it. Just like the black shirt, it hugged his chest and especially his thick biceps, but it fit. Samantha could only sigh. When she did, he turned to her and smiled slightly. A rush of warmth flowed through her, and since it yearned for perfection, she grabbed his hand and wrapping it around herself, she held him very close.

He lifted a hand, tentatively, haltingly, and brushed a wisp of hair away from her face. Samantha felt like a teenager all over again, in the arms of the very first boy to ever touch.

"How long?" she heard herself whisper.

"We take a walk and-" he paused, then set his lips.

"Walk. Then what, Kane?" she didn't want to push him too much though, and in any case, it seemed he was interested enough to invite her for a walk with him, rather than ravish each other and be done with it. Perhaps this is how it is with werewolves, she reasoned as they exited the apartment. To them, sex and emotions are too intricately woven together.

"It is unsafe," he said suddenly. Before she could say or ask anything, he continued, "We can't detach our inner feelings from the act of making love physically," as if reading her mind, he answered her.

"Why is it unsafe?" she asked as they entered the elevator, but he did not answer her. Samantha was learning to read him, even if just. If she probed, he would probably clamp up even more, and if pushed further, exhibit his earlier arrogance. Sighing, she indicated with a smile that she was contented. He did not smile back.

"Where?" she took his hand and allowed him to lead her outside. She didn't mind who saw them together. Also, it was early evening, the best time for a walk, she reasoned. Her mind surely needed it- suddenly she remembered Nelson. With an elated chuckle, she realized that being close to Kane made her forget Nelson just as she would have wanted to.

"Nowhere in particular," he answered her query.

"Okay." She sauntered comfortably beside him. It was that time of evening when everything seems abuzz with the expectation of night; vehicles zoomed past them, as if in a hurry to arrive at their destinations, people hurried in both direction, heads bowed, minds perhaps astir with thoughts of what to expect once in their respective homes. Nature had not been left behind too in this evening's buzz; crickets jostled for listeners with shrill notes, while cicadas flew about in concerted efforts to elude bats which were also out to hunt.

In the heavens, the bright moon and the dark clouds played a celestial game of their own; hiding, seeking and being discovered, and the moon's joy at being found gifted a fast darkening world with nostalgic lunar light.

Chapter 5

Kane was hungry. Of all the things he had experienced so far in this town, hunger seemed to debilitate him more. Recalling the place, he had been to earlier when he had woken up and found her gone, his stomach grumbled at the prospects of what awaited. He quickened his step-

"Hey, I thought we were together!" he heard the woman yell behind him. High above them, the moon hid once again and the dark clouds took over.

He slowed a bit to wait for her to catch up.

"I will eat first," he informed her, "The we will walk."

"Aren't we walking already?" she yearned to take his hand, but restrained herself. Better let him deal with his ravenous appetite. He didn't answer, for just then, they were in town. The sight of a place that would alleviate his tortured stomach was more than an enough incentive to make him forget that he was in the company of a pretty, but troublesome woman. Perhaps it is already closed, he thought, for it seemed too good to be true to his grumbling stomach. No, it was open. That was all his famished body needed. Once at the door, he seemed to regain a bit of control over his hunger; he opened the door and held it open for her.

"I don't believe it! Samantha?" Kane heard the shout and noticed someone rush from the counter and hurry towards them. A young man, probably younger than he had deduced Samantha to be met them and grabbed Samantha in a tight hug, followed by several granny pecks on both cheeks.

Next he turned to Kane, face nearly splitting from his wide smile, arms opened wide. Completely impervious to the young man's affability and sunny demeanor, Kane brushed past Samantha and her interesting, probably long lost friend, and hurried over to the furthest table from the entrance and sank into a seat. He chose the one facing the entrance where at the moment, Samantha and her weird friend oohed and aahed at each other. Kane observed them for a moment. Was he her brother maybe? The cheek pecking ruled that out, unless they were really close siblings. As a boy, Kane could barely stand any physical contact with his siblings, in whatever form, shape or kind.

Perhaps the young man was her ex-boyfriend then. But that seemed highly unlikely; the clothes she had given him, Kane, had been worn by someone taller. Or perhaps, a friend with benefits. Kane chuckled softly- in Hale, it was unheard of, friends with benefits. Still, it was possible here, Kane reasoned, and not unusual amongst humans. For some reason, his intuition signaled that Samantha was unmarried; previous relationships, perhaps, but not married. He wondered why the thought gave him so much relief.

He didn't care about all that though; he was here, and that was all that mattered, at least for the moment. He lifted his nose and drew in a deep breath; he felt that the food aroma wafting from the kitchen behind him was wasting away. It was better if he started with it by pleasuring his olfactory senses.

He hadn't noticed anyone approach, but suddenly someone was standing at his table, offering him a menu. He grabbed it quickly, scanning it and feeling that everything printed there was palatable. Whoever had handed it to him left with a promise to be back shortly to take his order.

In a moment, Samantha joined him. He glanced up once then buried his face into the menu once again. He addressed her though,

"I feel I can eat anything," he pointed at something. "I'll have that."

It took a moment for him to notice that she hadn't responded. He glanced- then took a double take.

"What's wrong, are you okay?" he sounded slightly alarmed as he scrutinized her. Her eyes were wet as if she had just been crying. He was shocked at the sudden change. From a forceful and assertive personality, there she sat opposite him, sniffing and dabbing at her eyes, looking lost.

"I'm fine, Kane. Just give me a moment..." she stood up and left. He gave it no more thought. Presently, the excited squeals emanating from behind the counter. Kane shook his head slowly, but did not turn around.

How humans process emotion is an enigma, he reasoned. From an apparently perpetually aroused woman, to a sniveling mess a moment ago and now she laughing gaily like a young girl with someone at the counter... he shook his head and leaned back in his seat to wait for his food. Philosophizing about humans was akin to merciless mental torture. The squeals increased in volume, and now she did sound truly happy. Still, Kane did not turn around. His attention was focused on three new customers who had walked in, all men.

He paid rapt attention to all their movements as he observed them select a table near the entrance. Applying his heightened senses did not reveal anything untoward about them that would have aroused his interest or caused him concerns, from their scents- they were humans- talk, and general body language.

However, Kane reasoned, someone from Hale could use humans to search for him. Suddenly, he felt the familiar contempt begin to well up within him. A uniformed girl whooshed by him as she went to welcome the newcomers and hand out the menus. As Kane observed them carefully, his mind recalled one of his deeply buried memories; no matter how hard he tried, he couldn't evict the recollection.

Elvara. That had been her name. Both of them had been young, and perhaps immature in terms of love, but no one could have dissuaded them nor kept them apart. No one did indeed, for it had been a secret. Open knowledge was that no werewolf and human had been in an intimate relationship, but Kane Knew better. Then, one sunny morning- he jolted suddenly as if electrocuted. The memory had awoken his instincts, and for a moment, he wasn't sure of where he was. The sight of a waiter weaving towards him tray in hand tamed his thoughts and calmed his instincts.

He could feel his canines receding- suddenly, the thought of turning without being in control seemed very real. It was an alarming prospect. Fortunately, no one seemed to have noticed his reaction to a memory of long past, now deeply buried but pressuring for expression.

"Not busy at this time of the day," Samantha observed quietly as she joined Avenue at the counter. From there, they could see the man she had brought in; he had the menu in his hands, but he didn't seem to be reading; rather, he seemed to be watching the door.

"So, anything I should know?" Avenue used the voice Samantha knew only too well. He wanted to know all about the man she had brought in, the man who had made her return to a place she had sworn never to set foot in.

"Not much really. Just a hungry out of towner looking for good food,"

Samantha filled her friend on what she knew, or really wished to reveal. Suddenly she realized that apart from what she had withheld from Avenue, indeed that was all she knew about the man; he was yet to reveal why he had been attacked by dogs, why he flinched at the sight of steaming liquids, or even his behavior the previous night when they had kissed.

Other than his name, and the fact that he was a werewolf, he had not divulged much else.

"Who is he?" Avenue persisted. With anyone else Samantha would have lost her patience, but she knew Avenue wouldn't let it go. She glanced at her friend. He was just looking out for her. He wouldn't rest until he was sure that Samantha was safe, hungry stranger or not. Friends like M'lyka and Avenue are rare to come by, she thought tenderly.

"I don't know," She replied truthfully. Avenue searched her face as he leaned against the counter and crossed his arms. Samantha just shrugged. It was true, she knew what Kane was, but she didn't know who Kane Limaric was. They remained silent for a moment, each ruminating on their thoughts while occasionally glancing at their focus of interest.

Since he sat facing the main entrance, Kane did not know that rather than out there in the streets, in here were two people who were very interested in finding out a bit more about him.

"But you came with him- potential interest perhaps?" Avenue broke the silence.

"No, Ave, no," she shook her head emphatically. Avenue smiled, then winked,

"Intense denial, Sam. You seem to be trying to convince yourself more than me."

"Please, Ave, not now. Please?" Samantha glared at her friend. Sometimes, even with the best of interest at heart, she felt that Avenue could be a pain and a bother, not unlike M'lyka. Just as her ire had risen, it dissipated, leaving her feeling awful.

"I didn't mean to snap at you, Ave," she bit her lip. "I just, I don't know…" Suddenly she remembered her earlier distress immediately after M'lyka's revelations about a rogue werewolf. Suddenly the possibility that Kane was a fugitive from the law seemed very real. Something else too that did not help matters, M'lyka knew what Kane was, and Samantha had told her. Damn that psychic! Samantha cursed silently, she led me on and observed my body language. Oh God! She clapped her hands to her lips, perhaps there is no female werewolf!

It was all a ruse to get me to reveal even more! She found herself observing Kane with renewed interest mingled with dread. What if- just at that moment, he turned around and smiled at her. She couldn't help but notice how long his canines were, or how dark his eyes seemed as they regarded her, as if he somehow knew.

"Are you alright?" Avenue's concerned voice brought her back to the present. She snapped out of it- Kane was still where she had left him, attacking a plate of beef, his whole focus on the entrance of the restaurant.

Samantha nodded to Avenue's query, then smiled. Had Avenue read her body language too? Samantha could not keep everything away from her friends, but before divulging anything, she would find out as much as possible about Kane. But not now, she decided. She couldn't talk about it just yet. Putting on a smile, she turned to Avenue.

"I'm okay, just fatigue, I guess. I've had an intense morning." She glanced at Kane - he was still seated, still checking the entrance. Not once did he turn to look behind him at the counter where two people who were very interested in him stood.

"Enough about me, Ave, what about you? Anything good happening?"

"Aw, Sam, just the same- there's a lot that's been going on since you left..."

"Tell me about you first," she cut him off. "We'll catch up on the rest when we get together- which is soon, I promise," she assured him when she noticed his face fall. Samantha and Avenue Parks had always been friends since college. Ostracized from a young age for his feminine mannerisms, Avenue had found a friend in Samantha and M'lyka.

It was a friendship that had weathered much, and even now as she searched his young face and felt a rush of affection, Samantha made a mental decision to make an effort to spend more time with her other best friend.

"Well," Ave smiled and looked at everything around them but her, "Antony came back..." and the squeals resumed.

The squeals behind the counter wafted in shrill waves over to where Kane sat, but they failed to find hospitality in his ears, for he was deep in thought. Fortunately, he had managed to suppress his earlier memory; he didn't intent to dwell on that any time soon; rather, he had a moment to recall.

He was yet to get over what had just happened at back at that woman's- Samantha's place- He reminded himself. I have to stop thinking of her as 'woman' and 'human', he chided himself. As he sat there facing the entrance just like he had done earlier in the day when he had come alone, he wondered what Samantha had in mind. A passionate ordeal, an orgy of bodies- then what?

Despite his pride, Kane had to admit to himself- she had done so much for him. If she hadn't appeared when she did... he shook his head and refocused his recollections to their kiss.

She had used very few words, but her body had been loud enough to tell him what she wanted, and he had rebuffed her so far. What was that nonsense he had told her about detaching emotions from the purely physical act of making love? Kane scoffed- then frowned.

He knew that wasn't the reason and was willing to admit it to himself, but would he be able to come clean and tell her the truth that tortured him with every breath in his body? He didn't want to explore the option. One thing he was sure of, he and she would make love sooner or later, it was inevitable.

His body ached for her. She yearned for him with her every word and motion. And yet- still- that demon in his mind. He couldn't have argued with most of her logic after rescuing him, and he couldn't rebuff her forever if he was to continue accepting her help. If anything happened to her- or to him for that matter- no, he wouldn't overthink about it, not while his mind was still reeling from what had happened during their earlier kiss. What if tonight she invited him to her bedroom, would he go? What would follow after that? It was too soon and too risky to think anything beyond the kiss, he decided, and yet he could feel his body react to the images filling his mind and the sensuous sensations coursing through him, at the mere thought of her soft closeness and sighed yearnings.

The prospects, he decided, were beyond what his mind could accept at the moment. Yet- he closed his eyes and tried to recall every single moment- yet, he was not loathe to the idea of sleeping with Samantha. The suddenness with which it was all happening was a bit disconcerting though, too fast for his mind to keep up with while still retaining a sense of control. Just then, the main focus of his busy mind slid into the seat opposite his, effectively blocking his view of the entrance. She was smiling, but his senses let him in on how tense and nervous she was.

"What is wrong?" he dabbed his mouth with a napkin and asked the question.

"Ah, well, nothing much," she brushed hair off her face and avoided his dark, piercing gaze.

"I'm okay, don't mind me at all," she waved a hand dismissively. "Just go ahead and eat. Don't let me keep you." She stood up again. Kane sensed a sinking feeling in his stomach as realization started to dawn on him. She must have found out something about him, something that true or false, was unsettling. If, he reasoned, she was still as interested as she had been earlier, she wouldn't have been staying away from him- she would have stuck with him, wearying him with questions and torturing him with her blatant hunger for him.

Kane did not want her to leave.

"Don't leave," he held up a hand. "Eat with me." She observed him for a moment, then sat back down. He resumed his eating then looked up and attempted a smile. She smiled back briefly, but it did not console him. Though she sat with him, it was evident she wished she was somewhere else. Did she find him no longer irresistible, he wondered with feeling. He wasn't willing to let her go yet.

"You can leave. If you wish to." He wiped his mouth and sat back. "You don't want to be here. You don't want to be around me."

"What?" she had a confused look on her face, but Kane could tell that he had deduced it correctly.

"Your eyes were wet. You were crying."

"That makes you think I didn't want to come?"

"Why else then? Enlighten me?"

"No, Kane, you enlighten me." She bristled, taking him slightly aback. He hadn't expected this. She sat back in her seat and folded her arms.

"You want to know what- something about me?" he asked her quietly.

"Yes, and more, Kane. Everything about you!" her eyes flashed, though her whole demeanor seemed to be softening.

"You know my name..."

Kane sensed a presence behind him. Looking up and around, he saw the same young man who had met them at the door hovering over them. Samantha smiled at her friend. Avenue moved closer, his eyes on Kane.

"I'm so sorry, Sam," the young man handed them a check, which Kane took. Still, the young man lingered. Kane, with resentment rising, reasoned that the young man must have set Samantha against him. Perhaps that was it. Looking behind him again, Kane glared at the younger man. The cursed fool must have fed her mind with nonsense, rumors- she had been okay on their way over, but suddenly, she had changed. And now here he stood by their table offering stale apologies, rather than giving the two a moment to mend whatever little they had woven together in the short time they had known each other.

The younger man barely noticed the other man glaring at him. He was laughing gaily at something Samantha had said. Kane cleared his throat once, then twice. Still the young man did not seem to be in a hurry to move. Feeling his frustrations begin to rise, Kane started to rise from his seat too. Samantha must have noticed the silent tension, for she put out a restraining hand. She nodded at her friend who left without another word. Kane sank back in his seat and regarded her coolly.

"Who is he?" he asked suddenly.

"My best friend," she answered tersely.

"Are you related to him? Does he work here?"

"Yes, he works here," Stacy answered simply. She had ignored his first question.

Kane felt that their curt exchanges were headed nowhere good, but he was beginning to feel his frustration rise. He had invited her for a walk, he had also invited her to sit with him, but she seemed to have changed. No longer was she smiling as much as before. She wasn't even playing with him by making him talk as she had earlier.

He should have left her that night and not accepted anything from her. Still, and he admitted this with dread, he wanted her close. He needed her more than he was willing to accept, even to himself.

It was the young man he didn't like, and even more when he thought that he could have ruined their moment with baseless rumors.

"Why did he make you cry?"

"Look, Kane," she said suddenly. "If you can't or won't answer half the questions I ask you, then please don't ask me anything."

"My questions have answers. Yours don't." he seemed unfazed at her sudden outburst.

"Are you jealous, Kane?" she asked suddenly.

"Jealous of what?" he asked incredulously.

"Avenue. You seem to be on his case all of a sudden."

"Who's Avenue?" Kane looked around them.

"My friend who met us at the door," Sam sighed in restrained exasperation at having to explain. "His name is Avenue." As she spoke he listened keenly and nodded slightly in understanding.

Suddenly, Samantha felt a stab of guilt for her outburst. She smiled suddenly, then attempted a laugh. "Those were tears of joy, seeing that we haven't seen each other for some time. The last time we saw each other..." she sighed and looked up as if to summon some painful recollection. "Was not so great. Just remembering it- oh, I'm so sorry," she dabbed at her eyes and smiled. "You must be wondering why I would be so bothered by such issues..."

"You shouldn't be around him then," Kane advised philosophically.

"He's my best friend, Kane. He's looking out for me."

"Why did he set you against me?" Kane heard himself blurt, and he couldn't control the snarl in his voice.

"Why- what?" The surprise on her face was genuine. "What has gotten into you? Why would he do that?"

"We came, you were glad in my company."

"My God! Kane! Arrogance, I can tolerate. Pride, that too. Insinuations, suspicions and baseless accusations, not that much!"

"You spoke to him, now I do not excite you any longer."

"Excuse me, excite?" She leaned towards him. "You talk of excitement, Kane? Aren't you the one preaching abstinence?"

"What are you talking about?" But he knew, and as he waited for her to vent her frustrations, he had a feeling that her foul mood had something to do with that.

"How many times does a woman have to throw herself at you? You've repulsed my advances, you were rude-"

"I wasn't... rude."

"And still are! You are arrogant, and you won't tell me what is going on with you! How am I supposed to react, huh?"

"I'm not rude. I was never rude. I have a proud heritage."

"Whatever Kane, or whatever your name is! I'm leaving."

"Not yet." He spoke so quietly, with so much confidence that she paused midway in rising from her seat and gaped at him.

"What?" she seethed at him.

"The walk. We came for a walk. We are yet to."

"I've walked enough!" She stood up. "You wanted good food when we first met, and you got it, and more. You are one heartless, thankless son of a-"

Just be glad that I took the time!" Her eyes blazed as she glared at him. He glared back at her darkly. He started rising from his seat when she moved.

"Don't follow me!" With a huff, she left the restaurant. Despite the severity of their argument, no one seemed to have noticed. If they had, no one seemed to care. Not even the young man, who suddenly appeared, a deep frown on his face.

"Where is Sam?" he asked Kane, who stood up slowly, counted some bills, placed them on the table and without a backward glance, left too.

Chapter 6

Night had landed, covering Green Bay like a dark but light blanket, and full of holes, and through these holes starlight was visible, twinkling, winking. Kane looked up at the heavens. Still unable or unwilling to think and process what had happened between him and Samantha, he walked slowly. What was he to do? He yearned to make her understand. The greatest dilemma was that, Kane was yet to understand, so, how was she expected to if he himself was afraid of it?

The night was still young. Sighing deeply, Kane made a sudden decision, one he decided he would stick by. Since he still had some of the money she had given him, he decided to buy clothes. Then he would return the ones she had given him, and that would reduce his debt to her. That, in turn would reduce the baggage in his mind.

With that resolve held firmly in his mind, he started hunting for a boutique that was still open. He would think through the rest of his current troubles as soon as he was done with the clothes, he decided.

Up to that moment she still didn't know how to make of her time with the werewolf from out of town. True, she had enjoyed herself immensely, certainly more than she had enjoyed herself for quite a while. She had also endangered her life; to her surprise, she was beginning to realize that the danger aspect gave the whole escapade with him a new angle, and it was this angle that gave the whole prospect such an adrenaline-fueled thrill.

It had been unplanned, one of those spontaneous moments that made such an incident worthwhile and even worthy of treasuring, as she was now by extending her hospitality. Had she been told that she'd meet a man at night by rescuing him and that he would make her forget her troubles, even for a few hours or days, she wouldn't have believed it. But it had happened.

Was it worth it? She felt that yes, given a chance, she would not hesitate to spend time with him again, despite his crude manners and somewhat inflated ego. She didn't know him, but wasn't that one of the reasons of spending time together, to get to know each other more? If she sought him, he'd interpret it as interest. She didn't know how that would go; she still didn't know what he was running away from, and for how long he planned to be in Green Bay.

There was the chance he would also be interested and would probably seek her company again, but she wasn't sure.

Kane had always been very guarded around women; human and werewolves. But whenever he was in dire need or in a difficult situation, they always seemed to be around. The moment he walked into a boutique, one was at his heels, just as he was contemplating abandoning the whole idea of buying clothes.

"Hi there," she greeted him with a wide smile. "Don't leave, we have your size- oh my-" she moved closer, hands outstretched as if to measure him by patting him, and Kane took two steps backwards. The woman lifted her hand in mock surrender, "No hands if it makes you uncomfortable," she assured him comfortingly. "What do you have in mind?"

Kane liked her smile. "A shirt, a pair of pants and a cardigan- like these ones," he indicated himself. "But not as tight."

"Oh, sure. We have something at the back, follow me please."

"I'll appreciate it if you pick them out and wrap them for me."

"Don't you want to try them out? It is not mandatory, but recommended," she smiled wider and beckoned. Kane, understanding that further resistance would arouse suspicions, followed her. As he did, he utilized his heightened senses since he didn't know where the next attack would come from. It was just at that moment he realized he felt safe around Samantha.

To his surprise, he realized that he missed her presence. Perceiving no danger in his vicinity, Kane relaxed slightly and even allowed a young assistant to take his measurements. Once done, the woman he had met at the door led him to a rack and assisted him to pick whatever he felt he needed. She was very patient as she advised him on color choice, as well as what went well with what.

Task accomplished, and after realizing that he was adamant about not trying them on, she led him to the counter where the same assistant who had taken his measurements wrapped his purchase. He paid and was hurrying towards the door when he heard hurried footsteps behind him. He whirled around- it was the woman, a receipt in hand.

"You never leave this," she admonished. "In case of a return or wish to exchange."

"Thank you." He took the receipt and resumed his exit.

"Hey," he turned around. She stretched out her hand. "Thank you for shopping with us. I'm Sarah Binds." Kane shook the proffered hand, then bowed slightly.

"Pleased to meet you Sarah. Thank you for your assistance." With that he exited the boutique.

I'll need a job, he thought suddenly as he walked. I'll need to find a way to pay Samantha back. He looked around him and observed other people as they passed him in both directions. *What kind of a job would I do here?* he wondered.

Most of the others who shared the young night with him on the street seemed to embrace a very wide spectrum; from unskilled labor to specific careers. He noticed some in unofficial garb, heavy backpacks supported on tired but still determined shoulders. He watched others in suits, briefcases in hands, faces set, and gaits tired but still determined. Very few cars were on the road- something he had noticed even earlier during the day. This town loved walking.

His mind took him back to Hale, where he had lived for most of his life. He saw himself as he had been back then, decked in a lab coat, tablet in one hand pen in the other, standing by while monolith engines whirled, roared, groaned and sometimes screamed as they did what they had been designed to do. And Kane, young, ambitious, blinded by the prospects of a dazzlingly bright future stretching in front of him had dedicated himself wholly. Life couldn't have been better. But, and he winced with the memory, backward traditions couldn't have been more cruel.

Hale was a megacity, but this was a small town, he reasoned. He doubted he would find any medical research facility comparable to the one in Hale, and even if he had he wouldn't really go asking for a job and yet he was expected to be in hiding. He also expected be in the town for a week at most. Then, he would be back to his own world. But would the problems that had seen him escape with barely his life be gone in one week? He didn't know and he wasn't ready to think about it at the moment. What would he do once back?

In Hale too much of one's life was sapped by hierarchical politics, and Kane loathed succession politics with a passion. Everyone seemed obsessed with titles and their place in society. They stole the focus from what mattered most.

To many in Hale, life was all about who ruled, who changed the rules, who was making the most impact in terms of superiority, be it physically, intellectually, and economically. He was tired of it all. To him, all that mattered was the world.

There was more than Hale, he felt and he had always felt it. He had held such ideas from a young age and more so after his first turning at the age of eighteen. A late bloomer his age mates had taunted him endlessly, but Kane had been unfazed for as time went on, he and the others too had come to realize that his lateness in turning had benefits, namely a strong mind and an unequalled logic in terms of reasoning.

This reasoning, he now reasoned as he crossed a street and hurried on, was what had caused him endless pain and heartache. And the name at the center of it all was Elvara, the girl he had met and loved... Kane felt his emotions begin to stir; he closed his eyes and shook his head vigorously, all in an effort to eject the memories that threatened to resurface.

No longer focused on any destination, he let his feet walk and his nose guide him. His mind didn't register that he was entering a building. Neither did it realize that he was in an elevator, but he knew that he wanted to go to the third floor.

His aimless wandering had brought him to her door. Kane hesitated as he went through his mind in an effort to find a justifiable reason as to why he was back at Samantha's. To thank her of course, he thought, and to- he needed to change, didn't he? He would thank her for all she had done, return the clothes she had given him once he had changed into the ones he had bought, promise to pay her back since he had used her money, and then leave her in peace. This wasn't his place, never was and apparently, never would be. With those decisions made, Kane knocked on the door.

"You've done so much," he started with feeling the moment the door was opened, "And- please understand- place yourself in my shoes for a moment." She stood there, her face unreadable. Suddenly, she opened the door wider and bade him to enter.

He did- and looked around him in the room. He glanced at her, then at the door as she closed it. True, this was Samantha who had opened the door, and he had pressed number three in the elevator, but- something was different.

"I rearranged the room," she filled him in, wiping the quizzical look away from his face. It was true. She had moved the larger couch he had spent the previous night on, from near the middle of the room, to the furthest corner, next to a bookshelf.

She must have been working on the books, he reasoned, for there were some on the couch and others on the floor. The table was not where it had been too, as well as the small desk, which was now flush against the wall by the door.

In the middle of the room, which was now empty she had placed a rug. His ears were not deaf too to the soft music emanating from somewhere in the room. "I do this whenever I'm upset or stressed." She added and started moving rhythmically, "Come, let's dance."

"I hunt." He contributed and noticed her frown. She opened her mouth, seemed to change her mind and closed it. She continued sashaying around while he stood in one spot, observing her. He realized he still had the package in his hands.

"What happened, what came over you suddenly?" Her voice lilted with the violin notes wafting from some spot he still could not locate. Kane glanced at her, as if unsure of what to do next. As if reading his mind, she danced over to where he stood and took his hand.

"Don't you wish to feel better?" Her voice seemed to be coming from somewhere else, not her. "Don't you want it all to be easier, clearer?" He did. Hesitantly, he started moving like she was, right foot forward, gentle twist of hips, right foot backward, another soft gyrate, swinging of hands as if to catch the wafting melody.

And slowly, almost unconsciously, Kane felt it all indeed getting better, easier, clearer. The music changed, transitioning seamlessly and effortlessly. As if on cue, the lights dimmed slightly, just as he felt his hand taken. She stood in front of him, eyes twinkling, body pliant and moving quietly with the music.

He followed her lead- when she held his shoulders, he held her waist, and the two bodies evicted the small gap between them. The soft music dictated, and the body, compliant to the yearnings of the mind, obeyed and moved accordingly.

"I'm enjoying myself," she rested her head on his chest, "I want you to, too."

"I'm taking so much from you," he whispered. "With nothing in return."

"You don't know that." He felt her move her hand from his shoulder to his back. They continued swaying, "Be silent, let it soak in."

"You spoke," he admonished as he stroked her hair. "And I reacted appropriately."

"Well," She smiled up at him. "Tell me you are not enjoying yourself." He did not answer- that is, verbally, for his mind had stepped back, leaving him at the mercy of his body. He pulled her closer till they seemed to meld into one weaving, fluid motion.

He was not sensually unaware of her quickened pulse nor her gentle but firm thrusting against his already tortured groin. He felt a strong urge to possess her, to do more than just dance. His body screamed for immediate relief- and before he could regain his mind in order to tame it, the release came, sudden and with fury.

He groaned as he turned. His canines elongated and his body form morphed so quickly, he had had no time to hide from the woman in front of him. The grey cardigan he had on was stretched taut to tearing point, while the pants had ripped in places- through which thigh muscles peeked through.

In a moment, where a second before danced a man was a werewolf, inches taller, red eyes glowing darkly, canines gleaming white in the dim light. The hands that had held the woman were now paws, thick, strong and sinewy. The werewolf change was complete. Regaining his mind, Kane held his breath and waited for the scream. It never came.

There are times when logic and reasoning seem redundant- and at such moments, intuition and emotions always take over-if allowed. Samantha had expected such a thing, and had been ready for it. Her intuition had been correct- after his weird behavior the first time they had kissed, and since he wouldn't talk about it, Samantha had taken some time to figure it out.

Whenever he got emotional, he covered it with brusqueness, sometimes arrogance, but she had seen through him, it seemed. And the music had served its purpose. Now to see what else it would uncover.

As the huge man-wolf stood in front of her, hesitant, domineering and yet- with a hint of fear in his obsidian eyes, Samantha took his hand- now paw- and resumed what they had been doing. He responded, but barely. Slowly, with settling dread, she watched as panic set in his red eyes as they lost their glow.

He will run off, she thought. She held him tighter as he resumed his human form, and did not let go, even when he tried to pry himself away from her grip. Suddenly she pushed him. He gave a surprised cry as he stepped backwards- tripped and lost his balance, just as she launched herself at him as he went down.

Kane yielded to the sudden aggressiveness as struggled to reason that it was his body still hangover from their dancing, that he had nothing to do with the sudden turn whatsoever. Soft lips assaulted as a determined tongue sought his mouth. He responded to the kiss, but just. His mind wouldn't let him. He heard her sigh in exasperation as she rose and moved away from him. In a moment, the music stopped and full lights resumed. Nothing could have put out the blaze in her eyes.

"What is wrong with you?" she screeched suddenly. "I'm more than willing- and I just proved that I'm not afraid of you! If you're not into women please tell me!"

He said nothing. He had risen too and stood there, regarding her with eyes that reflected a sort of turmoil in his head. She moved closer.

"What demons are you battling, Kane?" She attempted in placatory tones, though her eyes still flashed. "What is it?"

She stepped closer and looked up into his face. "Are you afraid of me? Are you running away from something?" At those words, a gasp escaped him, and a small smile formed slowly on her face.

"I know, I already suspected. Those weren't dogs that attacked you were they? They were your kind. Werewolves. What did you do, Kane?"

"Are you hiding something that you don't want found?" He did not answer. He walked over to where he had dropped the bag with the new clothes. Samantha watched silently as he exited the room and presently, she heard the shower running. Sighing sadly, Samantha sank onto the couch to bewail her luck, or lack of it.

Minutes later, Kane emerged from the shower. He had put on the new clothes. Samantha was still on the couch, and did not look up when he crossed over to where she was and stood close.

"I couldn't ask for more from you," he started. "You've done more than enough." She just shook her head without looking at him.

"I will get a job- a menial one, and pay you back," he continued. Still, she said nothing though she looked up and folded her arms.

"I'll leave." He turned towards the door. "Try not to be upset with me-"

Suddenly, Samantha rose and swung her hand. It was caught effortlessly.

"I don't ever want to see you again, coward," she seethed furiously, "Now let go of my hand!"

But he didn't let go. Turning around to face her fully, he narrowed his dark eyes as he searched into her hazel ones. Sam couldn't tear away from his gaze, and neither could she free her hand from his grip. With surprising speed, he pulled her closer to him and held her hand behind her. She could only groan in anticipation as he lowered his head, and she felt his lips brush hers.

She tugged at her held hand, but he didn't let go. She could feel his heart thump in his chest and his breath come out in quick gasps as he brushed his lips on hers once again. With her free hand, she grabbed him and pulled him closer.

The man was strong, for though he closed the gap between them, it was not because she had pulled him. Sam parted her lips and waited hungrily. When he lowered his once again, she grabbed his neck from behind and met his lips with a vengeance. She felt him trying to pull away, but she wouldn't let him. He would torture her no more.

She sought him with her tongue and finding his lips parted in invitation, she dove in. She heard him gasp as she explored him with her tongue. Feeling her captive hand released, she flung it behind his neck and with both hands around him, pulled herself up and around him, without leaving his mouth.

He steadied himself and caught her around the waist. Body aflame with desire and aching with need, Sam deepened the kiss and he responded in kind. She felt him begin to move. She closed her eyes and didn't open them until she felt herself being released. He had carried her to the bedroom and was now placing her on the bed. He let go of her waist, bit she didn't let go of his nape.

She held him tighter to draw him closer. He leaned over as she let him align himself over her aching body, his hard throb pressing onto her moist need. Suddenly, she felt that their clothes were in the way. Letting go of his neck, she began tearing at his new shirt. He in turn tugged at her blouse, and they both paused to chuckle when buttons popped and snapped.

Patience, unable to contain them abandoned them to their primal instincts, and the remaining clothing was torn off their bodies, to reveal steaming flesh. Gasping sharply at the pleasurable feel of his now unrestrained throb seeking for her pulsating invitation, she grabbed it and relished the audible gasp her touch elicited, accompanied by a soft snarl. He was well in control of his instincts, she could tell, for he hadn't shifted so far.

All the same she could feel the raw need in all his movements as he sucked her nipples, each in turn, before sliding out of her hand to go down on her. She lost control the moment his tongue found her pleasure spot.

He moved with precision, his motions well timed such that he did just enough to take her to the edge, but stopped just before she crossed over.

She grabbed his hair and drove herself into him, and he caught on her rhythm. Still, she wanted more. She moaned, writhed and cried with abandon, and still, she wanted more. With a loud cry, she yanked his head away from her center of pleasure, and pulled him towards her. She groaned uncontrollably when she felt his hardness between her thighs, sliding upward, upward, till finally it found its complement, pulsating with heat and wet impatience. The two, the pulse and the throb kissed each other before he slid in slowly, tauntingly. She was done with being teased. She drove herself towards him savagely, lifting her hips to meet his invasion with sweet fury and angry relief.

Pure pleasure, mingled with fiery passion and a yearning for sweet relief found expression in every inch of their bodies as they twisted, gyrated, buckled and jerked; in quest of relief and at the same time a thirst for more.

Nothing could have equaled the two love makers' bodies' spasms dance as well as vocal chords accompaniment when they finally found relief, when they finally made it to the peak of Mount Love. None had left the other, and none had lagged.

They both made it together as jolt after jolt of electrifying shivers animated them; closely followed by final delicious shudders as they uncoupled. Silence reigned for a while save for their rapid breathing, only to be broken by a hooting owl announcing the new triumph. The news were taken over by a cool breeze through the window, which then blew away letting the world know as it breezed.

The breeze made it to the park where despite the late hour was not empty of people. They all received it with smiles, some recalling their own such moments nostalgically, other shivering with future anticipation and expectation.

It breezed further, confidently, till it reached a large tulip tree. The tree rustled the information, and a figure standing beneath it snarled, and not in pleasure or happiness. It was the snarl of jealousy, a yearning for revenge.

Chapter 7

Morning came, and Samantha opened her eyes. Today was a working day. She had appointments, and she had unfinished projects. A workload awaited her in her laptop, and her phone's reminder buzzed with impatience, as did the alarm. Beside her he snored softly.

Recalling their night brought about a shiver of euphoria as she slid quietly off the bed and tiptoed to the bathroom. He was still snoring when she returned. Heavy sleeper, she thought as she walked out again. He was awake when she returned from the showers. She regarded him for a moment, a tentative smile on her face, and when he smiled back, she launched herself at him, disregarding the towel she had tied around herself.

This is heaven, she thought as she sought his mouth and he reciprocated. He did not reciprocate though when she dipped her hand into the covers and grabbed his morning glory.

"I believe you showered for a reason." He detached his mouth from hers to say it. "Job?"

"Urgh, did you have to remind me?" Her hand retreated from the covers, though her eyes were glued to the slightly nodding bump under the covers.

"I didn't, you woke up early." He pulled her close.

"Every word out of you is a mood killer." She pouted as he kissed her hair.

"What would you rather I said?" he murmured into her ear as he nibbled her gently.

"Unhh..." she murmured back, then grabbed him when she felt him detaching himself from her.

"No, don't stop!" She managed to gasp as he resumed his delicious torture. It didn't last long. With a gentle shove, he pushed her away from him and covered himself. "You do what you woke up to do," he chuckled slightly. "A job, I presume- oh!"

"What, what is it, Kane?" she asked in alarm at his sudden gasp.

"I need a job, too!" He flung the covers away, then retrieved them when he noticed her eyes on him.

"Please?" he begged.

"What, I can't see you naked?" Samantha laughed. "I am, and I don't mind!"

"I mind. Give me a moment please."

"As you wish, oh modest one. Let me grab a few things here." she selected a few items of clothing from the closet and left the room.

When he walked into the living room, she was sitting at her desk, tapping away at laptop keys, a deep frown on her face. She turned when she heard him enter.

"You work from home?" he asked.

"Sometimes. I have an office though. I'm supposed to be in today- damn! Why did it have to be today?"

"Something unpleasant about the day?" he asked innocently. She glanced at him, expecting to see perhaps humor or irony- he seemed serious.

"Were you married, Kane?" she asked suddenly, then regretted it immediately when she noticed the change in his demeanor.

"I'm, I'm not- don't accuse me of rudeness- I can't answer that. Sorry."

"Don't fret about it, I have closet issues, too," she consoled him and smiled effusively at the sudden change on his face. She started to rise from her seat.

"No, don't." He held up a hand. "I need to go find something to do. Anything, even cleaning cow pens."

"Well, if you are that serious- Avenue was complaining about lack of workers- but based on what happened yesterday, you might not like him that much."

"Your young friend in town at the restaurant?" he guessed, and correctly too, for she nodded.

"Do you mind unloading delivery vans?"

"No. Any job at the moment will do."

"What did you do previously? Or is that question also..."

"Medical research facility assistant." His lips were set, and she took it to mean he wasn't about to reveal more.

"I'll talk to Avenue." She picked up her phone, then dropped it as if it had scorched her hand. "Or, you can once you get there. Just tell him I sent you. He'll hire you on the spot."

Kane had noticed the sudden change in her demeanor and the terseness in her voice when she had dropped her phone, but as usual, he did not express interest. Friends fight all the time, he thought as he headed for the door.

"Thank you, Samantha Binds-" He paused suddenly and turned to her. He seemed to mull what he was about to say for a moment, seemed to change his mind and opened the door.

"Will I see you tonight?" she asked quietly.

"If I make it till then." He closed the door behind him.

Bless M'lyka. When Samantha finally made it to the office, she found her friend already there, in Samantha's office, seated at her desk, speaking in a placatory tone to someone on the phone.

"She's here, I'll let her know," she assured the person at the other end then replaced the receiver. Placing her elbows on the desk, she touched the tip of her fingers together and turned to Samantha,

"May I help you? Samantha is not taking calls today."

"Quit it, M'lyka," Samantha smiled at the humor. "Thank you for doing this."

"You are not picking up calls, clients are fuming, you have an appointment at-" M'lyka glanced at the digital clock on the desk. "Forty minutes ago."

"Oh God," Samantha groaned as she dropped into the only other chair in the office. "Do I need this?" She waved her hand around. "Do we really need this unpleasantness in our lives?"

"Yes, Samantha, you need it. Otherwise how will you feed him?"

"What?" Samantha seemed confused.

"The wolf in your house, Sam!" M'lyka's voice rose. "He needs to be fed!"

"Shhh!" Samantha shushed her friend shrilly, "Not so loud! What is gotten into you?"

"Nothing. What about you? What has been getting into you?" she asked it pointedly, and Samantha was not amiss to the insinuation.

"You've been on my case for a while now, M'lyka, why?"

"You're harboring a werewolf Sam! Have you found anything about him- except his powers in bed?"

"Those are insinuations, M! I never told you he was- that!"

"Well, Sam, your body tells more than your words do." M'lyka stood up and walked around the desk. She crossed over to the mirror on the wall and spoke as she checked herself. "Here's what I know so far; a werewolf on the run, he and my best friend have already..."

"You know nothing," Samantha interrupted her abruptly. "You don't know *anything*."

"Tell me what happened then," M'lyka bobbed up and down as if standing on springs. "You were flushed when you came in."

"It's chilly outside. And I rushed here and sweated." Samantha avoided her friend's dark, searching eyes. Hugging herself, she shivered, "Can't you feel it?"

M'lyka smirked her lips and looked out the window. "Indeed Sam. Cold weather can make you sweat. Now." She sat on the desk, facing Samantha. "You can't fool me. Something happened, I can tell."

"I just met him, M'lyka, and you found him on my couch. Besides, I'm not interested in anything at the moment," even as she said it, she wondered if she was trying to convince herself more than her friend.

"Perhaps he's the rogue," M'lyka mused. "Killed someone-"

"He is not!" Samantha heard herself blurt out suddenly. M'lyka had a very strange look on her youthful face as she scrutinized her closely. Samantha didn't like the look in her dark eyes.

"You reveal more and more," She twiddled a pen as she spoke, "Did you and him-?"

"I'm saying nothing else," Samantha crossed her hands, "You seem to know everything."

Opening her eyes wide, M'lyka moved back to where she had been siting and drew in several deep breaths.

"Sam," she whispered, "are you ready for the storm?"

Samantha didn't answer, well, not verbally, but her body language was sufficient to draw even more worried sighs from her friend.

Now there was no going back. Only the truth could bring M'lyka to her side- well, until she decided where she wanted it to go with Kane. And the truth meant giving her friend a dose of her misery. Drawing in a deep breath she stood up and walked over to the same mirror M'lyka had used earlier. She spoke without looking at her friend.

"Do you remember Kurt, M?"

"The architect you met in one of your projects, yeah," M'lyka answered, "What about him?"

"It was a rebound thing; I was still hurt about..."

"Darren, yeah."

"Well, brace yourself. We went to the movies." She turned slowly, almost dramatically and looked at her friend. "Then a concert later."

"Something's up," M'lyka started rising, but Samantha indicated that she remain seated. "It is better if you were seated for this," she warned her. She drew in a deep breath.

"We watched 'Groups of Five' at the theater and later attended the Grant Feelers lakeside show," she added and pretended nonchalance. She held her breath and waited for the reaction- and got it. She had expected a reaction, but not 'The Reaction'. It took but a moment.

"Oh God!" M'lyka screeched suddenly, startling her more than she had been ready for.

"You what?!" She screamed, then started moaning. "I missed that movie and the Grant Feelers concert because of a pact with you! Sam!" She rose abruptly.

"M'lyka, I'm sorry!" Samantha hiccupped with suppressed laugher despite her friend's agony at the revelation. "I decide to be truthful and this is how you react! See why I didn't want to talk about Kane?"

"Please, not now," M'lyka looked genuinely dejected. "I missed that show..." she whispered hoarsely as she sank back into her seat. "My idol, my life... Oh God! Why did this happen to me?!"

"M, stop it, please? He'll hold another one soon... perhaps..." Samantha tried consoling her friend. She looked at her as she sat there, rocking and moaning as if she had received the worst news ever. To her it perhaps was. She felt bad; she had meant to ruin M'lyka's mood just as she had ruined hers, but if her reaction was genuine, then perhaps Sam had ruined more than that.

Samantha crossed over and walking behind the desk, patted her shoulder. M'lyka shrugged her hand away then looked up at her. She was truly dejected, the tears rolling down her face in thin rivulets.

"Grant does only one lakeside show Sam, and you know that!" she sobbed. "One show a year! Did you know that it, do you know that?"

"Seriously? No. Truthfully- I, well, Kurt invited me, and... it just happened. I found myself there." M'lyka remained inconsolable. Shrugging away her friend, she lay her head on the desk to hiccup away the betrayal. Sighing, Samantha resumed her seat.

"M?" Sam tried. M'lyka just shrugged without looking at her. Samantha drew in a deep breath, for only one thing could placate her friend. "M'lyka? If you don't answer I won't tell you what happened last night."

"You slept with your wolf," M'lyka did not look up, "It shows on you."

"Not that. Something else. Something very confidential-" At that word, M'lyka lifted her head and glared at her friend.

"What could possibly be more risky, more foolish, and more suicidal than a human sleeping with a werewolf? You know, Sam. I'm yet to wrap my head around just that."

"Wait, M, didn't you tell me you would love to try it too? What is so different about me realizing it?"

"Mine is a fantasy to be immortalized on canvases and safely locked away. Yours is well- one of the most outrageous things I've ever heard. My God! Sam!"

"Don't give me that holier-than-thou look! You wouldn't have resisted too if it was you."

"Oh, but I would have, Sam. Unlike you, I never switch off my common sense!" Suddenly her face started crumpling up again,

"You went to that concert... you and him..." she started wailing again, but Samantha cut her off.

"If I tell you something, will you stop your whining? Will you give up the tantrums?"

"You just want to quip my curiosity. Nothing could possibly make up..."

"He turned into a werewolf. In front of me."

The reaction was immediate. M'lyka scrambled up and wiping her eyes, presented a comical sight as she tried smiling through her teary face. She grabbed a book and the pen she had been holding earlier. Then she turned to Sam, eyes sparkling with excitement.

"I want details, every turn and twist, including the creepy!" she spoke breathlessly, book open, pen poised to start sketching. "Another painting coming up! Yes! She pumped her fists in joy, then grabbed her friend suddenly. "How did it start?"

Samantha drew in a deep breath and started talking.

Samantha had been right about her young friend Avenue-when Kane arrived and asked for a job, invoking Samantha's name in the process, he was led to the back of the restaurant. Behind the building was a parked van. Several men were offloading several wooden crates.

"Okay then," Avenue turned to Kane, all business-like. "Those crates need to move from there, to there-" he pointed at a specific spot close to a locked door. Kane nodded.

"It's perfect, I'll help them." With that, he joined the men and started helping carry the crates to the spot Avenue had indicated. Avenue watched for a moment, then left.

As he worked, Kane found himself thinking of Samantha. He recalled her face vividly, and every time he replayed the events of the previous night, he sensed a familiar yet unfamiliar warmth within him. Where exactly this feeling emanated from he couldn't pinpoint, but he found himself, not once or twice, placing his hand on his chest, right where his heart thumped.

Damn your lack of exercise Kane, he chided himself as he felt the calluses start to form in his hands. He was quick, but the other men, accustomed to the job, were quicker. By the seventh round, he was sure he would drop if he did not stop for a moment to rest his aching arms. But then he was determined to see the day through.

"Don't sweat it too much," a deep voice startled him as he held onto a crate he and another man had just carried. The man had gone for another one, leaving Oliver to draw in his breath in gasps and to watch his sweat drip to the ground. He looked up and through blurred vision saw a dark face smiling down at him. Wiping the salty sweat off his face, he stood up on shaky legs and attempted a smile.

"Thanks," he started walking, the other man beside him, "I'll get used to it."

"Good one, that Esther," the man grinned.

"Who is Esther?" Kane asked. The calluses, tender, round and painful, burned when he looked at the remaining crates.

"She owns the hotel." The other man updated Kane. "You haven't met her? Great woman," he added wistfully.

"No," Kane answered truthfully. "I got the job form the young man..."

"Ah, yeah. Good for you then." The other man gazed at the distance distractedly, then shook his slowly. Observing him furtively, Kane realized that perhaps the man was besotted, or even in love with this Esther he had mentioned.

"Well," he clapped his hands suddenly. "Lots of crates to carry! On to it!"

"Unh..." Kane groaned, then attempted a smile when he noticed the other man looking at him with a hint of concern.

"You don't need to push yourself man," he placed a hand on his shoulder. "Take a minute, recover a bit. You are not used to this work, I can tell."

"I am good. I can carry a few more," Kane replied while flexing his aching arms. The other man regarded him for a moment, then shrugged, but with a smile.

"Just don't stress yourself if-" he shrugged again, then took hold of a crate. Kane nodded and drawing a deep breath, took hold of the other side of the crate. Immediately he stood up, his shoulder, bicep, back and hand complained with an aching, burning sensation. They walked a few feet...

he closed his eyes and gritting his teeth, renewed his determination to make it. He didn't make it halfway.

"Let's change sides," he panted. The other man acquiesced without complain. His other hand fared no better. By the time they made it, he was near staggering. The other man helped by hefting the crate and placing it where it was supposed to be placed on his own- while Kane sank onto the ground to catch his breath, and to let his body, unused to such labor, make sense of what had just happened.

Every muscle screamed with a burning sensation. Looking at his hands, he nearly screamed; the palms were raw, and several of the just-formed calluses had burst. The skin underneath was painful once exposed to the air.

"Don't peel them," the other man was standing over him. He looked around and sighting an empty crate, picked it and placing it near Kane, sat. "That was the last crate, he indicated as two other men brought another one and placed carefully close to the others.

"Sorry, name is Oloo," the other man held out his hand, then pulled it back. "Must be painful," he pointed at Kane's hands.

"Kane. Pleased to meet you Oloo." He pronounced it 'O-low.' Kane smiled through his agony, and slight worry. Though he winced, it was not from pain as much as it was from his hands mending. He held them in such a way that his new-found-friend would not notice as the open sores disappeared and the calluses softened.

"Same here. We used to use gloves but then..." Oloo held up his own hands. "We got used to it. You must not be used to such work. Your hands cracked up too fast."

Kane remained quiet for a moment, his mind abuzz. Owing to the reasons for his being there in that small town, he felt that he couldn't trust everyone, at least not just yet. But then, everyone he had met had been pleasant, helpful and affable. Was it fair for him to hold back too much? It would surely raise suspicions. Looking at Oloo sitting next to him as they caught their breath, Kane decided that he had to let something out, not much, just enough- and true, to allay any suspicions.

"I from out of town," he explained. "Looking for some quiet moments here." He waited with dread for Oloo to follow up with more questions.

"It happens," the other man merely nodded as he looked out into the distance. "Welcome to Green Bay." And that is how Kane got to know the name of the small town he had sought refuge in. Oloo stood up and held out his hand.

Kane gave him his - too late he saw the frown form on the dark man's face as he pulled him up. He held his breath and waited for the other man to panic, or perhaps raise the alarm, but Oloo merely smiled.

"Welcome brother," he whispered. "Not everyone is against you." He looked around them then turned back to Kane again. "This evening, at the park. Nathan."

With that he turned and hurried off without a backward glance. A moment later, Kane heard the van start and drive off. So far, he had encountered friendliness. Now a fellow werewolf- for that was what he was, Kane had no doubts- had befriended him enough to pass a message. If Oloo had found him, who else knew, friend or foe, discounting his two attackers that night?

Suddenly, he frowned as a thought struck him; could it be a ruse, a trap? Maybe. But Nathan? His old mentor and father figure? Kane was inclined to ignore the whole thing, but he knew he could not; it would nag him all day till he got closure. Trap or no trap, he would find out. In any case it was obvious that others knew where he was. Suddenly, he thought of Samantha. It brought a feeling of warmth inside him, but it was not enough to erase the disquiet within. Perhaps they knew where he had spent his two nights. Perhaps they had seen him with her. The thoughts were unsettling.

Hearing his name called, he looked up to see a woman standing at the door, eyes squinted against the bright morning sunlight.

"Hungry yet?" She asked him. She sounded too pleasant, he thought. Better be wary from now on, he decided as he stood up and smiled briefly. "No, not yet. Just thirsty."

"Come in, then." With that she turned and retreated back inside. Kane realized his heart was hammering. Was she one of them too? Breathing deeply to retain a calm demeanor, he entered and found himself in what looked like a storage room. Presently, the same woman who had called him reappeared, pitcher and glass in hands. Kane took the glass and held it as she filled it. He gulped the water thirstily and held out the glass, indicating more. She acquiesced and he drank all, but slower this time. When he lowered the glass, she was smiling. He reciprocated, but briefly.

"Next job is opening those crates containing perishables, which you will bring in here and arrange accordingly- in there." She pointed at a closed door that seemed to have fogged on the inside. Kane realized it was a freezer room. He nodded. "Afterwards you may take a break as well as eat." With another smile she left. Kane set himself on the assigned task, pushing out all thoughts that may have interfered with his focus. It was still early, he decided, and night would come. Then, he would face whatever waited for him out there.

"Is the beef gyro ready, Avenue?" Esther asked when she saw Kane enter the restaurant. Kane wondered how she could have known what he preferred, but he said nothing. Perhaps Avenue had told her, owing to the fact that it was the only thing Kane had had all this time.

"The food is here," Avenue announced. Kane's stomach acknowledged the delicious-smelling food by rumbling so loudly, just as the plates were placed in front of him.

The food was great. Kane bit, chewed, slurped, bit again, then burped, but politely. Suddenly he seemed to recall that he was not alone. It was not a busy hour, but still... he had manners, and he intended to apply them wherever he was. As the food settled comfortably in his stomach and released his mind to think of other things besides hunger, he found himself thinking about Samantha. For the first time he allowed himself to focus on her by recalling her dark hair which she sometimes tied up in a ponytail, but mostly preferred to let it down.

He thought of her hazel eyes which sometimes flashed with frustration. He thought of her laughter when she had been happy around him, as well as her tears the night he had knocked on her door and she had broken down... Kane felt that his mind was ready to dwell on how beautiful the woman really was.

He hadn't been that keen, he realized. Blame the attack, the constant hunger, the apprehension before he could express himself openly, the- he paused in his thinking, and his eating. I have feelings for her, he realized with a gasp. I'm falling in love with Samantha Binds. The realization gave him more worry than his earlier interactions with Oloo, the man who had seemed to recognize what he was.

Suddenly, he realized that someone had spoken to him.

"What did you say?" he resumed eating, but not as fast as before. The food had lost its taste.

"I asked if you were okay," It was Avenue, standing close by. "You seemed to switch off for a moment there, I thought you were choking."

"I'm good. Thank you." He covered his mouth with his napkin and burped again. The napkin though was to hide his canines, for they had lengthened slightly. Suddenly Avenue slid into the seat opposite Kane, who frowned slightly. He was yet to feel any fondness for Samantha's young friend.

"How is she?" Avenue asked, or whispered rather. Kane looked at him long and hard, then sighed.

"Who, Samantha Binds?" he asked quietly.

"Yes, Sam," Avenue answered him- since he faced the counter, he kept glancing that way, as if he did not want to be discovered- Kane leaned back in his seat as his mind whirled. Samantha had told him the young man was her best friend. When they had last spoken, Samantha had cried, and Avenue had apologized, though Kane had not been too keen to find out what had happened between them.

"She cried when she met you," he probed into the younger man in a cold voice. "And we exchanged unpleasant words later."

"I gathered," Avenue sighed- and Kane experienced a slight tinge of sympathy at his fallen face. Suddenly, Avenue jumped up and Kane glanced behind him. Esther had reappeared. Avenue leaned close as he made a show of picking up the cleared plates. "She blames herself for a childhood accident that killed her father," he whispered with emotion. "It is a lot to take in. Please try to understand her."

"I do," Kane defended himself from the thinly veiled accusation in Avenue's voice. "I try to."

"Tell her I'll be at the park this evening," he whispered as he walked away with the empty plates. "She won't pick up my calls. She likes you a lot, perhaps she'll listen, I think." He hurried off with the plates before Kane could say anything, just as Esther appeared by his table, coffee pot in one hand, two mugs in the other. The coffee was steaming.

It took so much effort to stifle the panic rising within him, as well as superhuman control to contain himself as he felt his canines begin to lengthen and his body begin to change.

"Coffee?" he heard her voice and he shook his head vigorously. If she continued standing there- he could feel his clothes tightening around him as his body reacted- but suddenly, she was gone, and through his confusion, dread, fear and panic, he heard her ask someone a few tables away.

He sighed with heavy relief as he felt his body relax and his canines recede. Had the woman noticed? He didn't know. Had anyone else for that matter? It was too risky, he realized. She could have placed the mug in front of him and poured the coffee without asking. He shuddered at the thought as he did not want to imagine what would have followed.

"I noticed you flinch earlier, when I brought coffee," the voice startled him. It was Esther. He hadn't heard her approach. He checked with dread- no, she didn't have the steaming coffee pot any more. She held a pitcher of water and a glass.

"I don't pry," she placed the glass on the table and filled it as she spoke. "We all have our quarks, fears and phobias." She smiled at him. "It won't happen again."

"Thank you," he picked up the glass and relished its coldness. "I'm being careful that's all."

He turned to look behind him as Avenue approached a tray in hand. He looked at the empty glass then at Kane and then Esther. She merely shrugged while Kane just avoided looking at him.

Kane couldn't help associating his earlier distress with the younger man's presence. Avenue placed the tray on the table immediately next to theirs. and started serving a couple who sat there. Service accomplished, he started clearing Kane's table. Suddenly, Esther took the tray from his hands.

"Let me help you with those," she said as she picked up the glass and water jug. Avenue surrendered and wiped the table clean. He looked up at the retreating Esther, then turned to Kane, urgency in his voice,

"Forget what I told you," he whispered hoarsely. "She'll only hate me for it." Kane was about to say nothing, but a sudden thought hit him. He turned to Avenue.

"Who is Sarah Binds?"

"What, how do you know her?" Avenue hissed and intensified his cleaning of the table. He no longer glanced up to check whether Esther noticed them or not.

"Pay Samantha a visit, tell her what you know," Kane stood up slowly. "Excuse me, I need to resume working." Avenue moved to let him pass.

"Sam will hate me for this," he spoke so quietly, as if to himself. "She'll never forgive me." Kane wasn't listening. With a slight bow, he exited the front of the restaurant through a side door and once again found himself in the back.

"Kane," he heard his name called. He turned- it was Esther, standing at the door he had just exited through. "Come," she beckoned, and he obeyed. She was standing outside the freezer room, looking at him with a look he couldn't begin to fathom.

"This is between us," she started, and Kane heard himself groan inwardly. Did everyone here harbor secrets that needed confidential whispering? *What now*, he wondered, another night rendezvous at the park? But that wasn't it. What Esther told him blotted out all the other whispers he had heard that day.

"Galou is around," she whispered. Kane felt everything begin to spin around him. A deep silence fell around him suddenly, save for a ringing pitch in his ears.

He grabbed his head and closed his eyes to still the dizzying whir, while Esther continued in hushed tones, "Don't bother finding out who I am or how I know this, or even how I recognized you the moment you came in," she admonished him. "Just know that not all believe you are guilty."

Kane could only groan in genuine pain. Esther was still speaking, "We know all about rules and all, but is it worth it if she finds where you're staying? This is Galou Kane. I know you wouldn't endanger a human life intentionally. The woman you're staying with- Samantha" at the mention of her name, Kane looked up briefly, agony contorting all his facial features.

Esther continued, "She's impetuous, assertive, well-intentioned; but, still a human- ruled by emotions more than reason. Right now I believe she's too besotted to see reason and- let you go."

"What?" He croaked painfully as all the memories of his time with Samantha left him through his heavy sighs that chocked him and brought tears to his eyes. In the memories' place he felt a deep yaw of emptiness that ached form suddenly, as a reminder of what he now considered a past to be forgotten, all because of that name, Galou.

She placed a hand on his shoulder, and he uncovered his face. "Go back to Hale, prove them wrong. Galou will follow you- at the moment she's a danger as long as you're here."

With that she left him trembling in the warm midday sun, his mind a jumble of thoughts and questions he couldn't begin to find expression for. None of them had noticed anyone slip away, having listened to every word.

Chapter 8

Samantha waited, and when she could wait no longer, left the apartment. She had come home early. She had prepared a delicious meal that could have turned the best chef in the world green with envy. She had danced alone while she waited. He had not come. Evening had set in and night was closely behind.

Sighing with disappointed worry, she had tried to convince herself that he was safe, he had worked late, he had decided to take an evening walk- but at the back of her mind, she kept recalling his words as he had left that morning. *If I make it till then*, he had said. Still she wouldn't call Avenue.

She suspected he had news she wasn't ready for, news that needed her to be better prepared. She thought of taking her phone with her, but shrugged at the last moment. *Avenue will nag too much*, she decided. For now, she wanted to find Kane.

***

Life is not fair. The thought kept playing and replaying in Samantha's mind as she walked. Why was happiness so elusive? Why was it so easy to get hurt all the time? Was this how life was supposed to be?

The street was lit, but empty of movement. She yearned to see a fellow human, for the loneliness and the silence, for not even a car sounded, even from far off. Too quiet, she thought, then realized that it was indeed too quiet.

Where were the people? Where were the cars, zooming past, lights dancing as if trying to tantalize? Suddenly she saw a car in front of her, a very decrepit car. Its doors hung crookedly on rusted hinges, and its hood barely covered a very rusted engine. The contraption rocked violently and from inside came vicious snarls and painful groans. Suddenly she heard her name called- and suddenly, a figure burst out of the car and rushed towards her. It was Kane, and he looked injured. He fell just as he reached her- and Samantha screamed.

"Sam!" strong hands gripped her shoulders, "Sam! Snap out of it! Sam!" She heard a sudden crack followed by sharp pain on her cheek- "Sam, it is me!"

Samantha stopped struggling just enough to see a very concerned face peering worriedly at her.

"Ave!" she cried in relief as she hugged her friend and looked about her. People walked, some fast, some slowly, cars zoomed past and the night which was just beginning to set in was full of nocturnal sounds. Samantha stared at her friend, who gazed back at her worriedly.

"What happened Sam- why would you cross the street with such recklessness? I nearly knocked you down!" Avenue spoke breathlessly. His young face was contorted with concern and thin sweat shone on his forehead. He led Samantha towards his car, a dark blue Passat and opened the door.

"I'm fine, Ave," Samantha tried to assure him. "I was just going to meet Kane," she added as she resisted getting into the car. Avenue sighed and closed the door when he realized she was determined.

"Sam- you have to talk about it, you know that." He held her hand. "There's evidence that you were not to blame- and you can't run forever."

"But not now, not here," Samantha frowned furiously. Avenue frowned back.

"Why, Sam?" he tried desperately. "Why are you torturing yourself? Don't you want closure?" Samantha remained quiet for a while as if mulling his question which she considered to be rhetorical. Drawing a deep breath and feeling very calm, she turned and faced him fully. Avenue crossed his hands and waited.

"Ave," she started then paused as if rearranging or sorting through what she wanted to say, and what not to. "Listen Ave. I suspect you may have found out something about that day but please understand- I am not ready for the emotional upheaval just yet. How old was I, ten, eleven? Please Ave."

She placed a hand on his chest and looked into his eyes. She felt a stab of guilt at how tortured with concern and worry he looked, but she couldn't, she simply couldn't deal with what he had to say at the moment.

"It's not your fault," he whispered then grabbed her hand when he noticed the guardedness in her eyes. "It was an accident, Sam..."

"Oh God, Ave!" she screeched suddenly, "I'll tell you when I'm ready to talk! Please don't say anything else or- if you have to talk, tell me Kane got a job there."

"Well, but Sam-"

"I'm warning you, Ave! I'll leave you here!"

"Well- okay, he did, and he worked the whole day. He left two or three hours ago- but..." He stopped suddenly and Samantha grabbed him as if to shake it out of him. This was Kane they were talking about, and at the moment he mattered, certainly more than relieving regrettable childhood memories that could not be undone.

"He seemed disturbed- please this is between us Sam- Esther told him something and he left soon after."

"Did she fire him?" Samantha fumed. "Did they quarrel or something?"

"Well, no. She treated him as if she knew him, though he betrayed nothing on his part. When they last spoke, she mentioned- I'll get fired for this Sam. They seemed pretty intense, the two of them, like it wasn't mean to be heard by anyone else."

Slowly, Samantha felt a nasty sinking feeling begin in her chest and spread to her stomach, to settle in cruel hard knots. Suppressing a sob, she began walking. She did not stop, even when she heard Avenue calling her. She did not look back.

I should have known it, she thought savagely as hot tears burned her eyes and trickled in salty rivulets down her cheeks. *I should have known it!*

So Kane had found comfort in the arms of another woman! Of all women - Esther! She tried to suppress angry sobs as she walked on, not caring where her feet took her. She had a mind to go to that restaurant and confront Esther, but what would she tell her? Accuse her of stealing Kane from her with deceit?

Samantha was sure that was what it had been - deceit. Badmouthed her to the one person she had more than connected, the one person she had experienced something deeper than just lust. With an angry sob, Samantha realized that she had fallen for Kane. Whether he felt the same she didn't know, but- nothing mattered any more. He was gone, he had left her.

Samantha sobbed dejectedly as she walked angrily, stomping feet left to decide where they wanted to take her, since she no longer cared. Behind her, a worried Avenue followed from a safe and concealed distance.

She walked and soon found herself at the park. Her mind must have directed her there, for she could not recall consciously deciding that that was where she wanted to be. Night had settled cozily, and despite her current dilemma, Samantha took a moment to let her inconsolable mind take in the park after dark.

Even in the dark, the place was mesmerizing. Devoid of artificial lights, what little natural light there was gave the place a dark, solid presence that felt eerie. Unlike the streets, the park was quieter. The only movement was from the trees communicating through constant breezes and bats that darted silently about. The only sounds were crickets and cicadas as they competed in shrill notes contest.

Feeling her earlier agony chase away her silent appreciation, she reoriented her senses and headed for the grove. This was a place near the southeast end of the park. Several trees had formed a sort of a rough circle, and their branches had formed a canopy high above. It was a deliciously cool place during the day, but at night is was very dark.

That is just what she needed, a very dark place to sit in and sort her likewise dark thoughts. She arrived at the grove and headed for a large, fallen log, on which she sat. Barely had she settled when a shadow appeared.

"Don't scream! It is only me!"

Samantha felt her initial alarm turn to sour annoyance. "Avenue?" she screeched, "You followed me?" He moved closer- she felt him patting the air around him and feeling the log, he sat.

"I did not invite you," she retorted furiously.

"I know. I'll leave if you ask me to." He spoke quietly, without feeling. Feeling a sudden stab of guilt, Samantha felt around and found his hand. She took it and sighed.

"Just don't talk," she squeezed his hand and heard him gasp, "about anything."

"Okay," he groaned back. They remained so for a moment, each busy with their own thoughts. Presently, he stood up.

"I'm pressed," he replied to her unasked question. "I'll just be a moment," he told her as he left the grove. "Don't move."

"So fast?" she asked when she sensed a presence close to her. "Please don't tell me you just watered a bush." Avenue did not answer.

"You have my mate," a quiet voice seethed in her ear. Sam screamed.

***

"Who would try such a thing?" In another part of the park were two tall figures, conferring earnestly.

"Who knows?" The elderly of the two shrugged. "But you must come back Kane. Prove your innocence. Your running away will only make things worse for you. And for us. Think of Oloo and Esther, risking all they have so carefully build in this town, just because- we are looking out for you, risking our lives..." The old man trailed off with emotion.

"You saw what happened the last time I was there, Nathan. I was attacked. I escaped and on my first night here, I was attacked again and nearly killed. Listen," Kane placed a hand on the elderly man's shoulder. "I am innocent, but I have no way of proving it at the moment. The only way would have been through my eyes, but you know what those rogue doctors, supported by corruption and a thirst for quick profit did!"

"I do, I get you completely," Nathan nodded slowly. "Rarely do you see blue eyes in werewolves anymore- the only sign of guilt. Those doctors are surely turning up profit, if they can indeed do something to make the guilt innocent by just changing the color of their eyes."

"So, tell me Nathan, how else am I supposed to prove that I killed no one? How else am I supposed to face a whole nation turned against me?" Nathan remained quiet.

"I'll need evidence. I'll look for it, it doesn't matter where- and once I do get it I'll come and I'll face the Council of Ethics. But not before I have evidence."

"How are you that gathering evidence?" Nathan asked, "By spending time romping with a human?" Kane detected a hint of contempt in the old man's voice. Suddenly, he felt a strong dislike for his mentor.

"What are you talking about?" Kane stepped closer to the older man, his words accompanied by a faint snarl.

"Word travels. You may be innocent, but you risk so much if you have anything to do with..."

"There's nothing!" Kane heard himself flare suddenly. "Have you been spying on me? That O-low? Esther? Others I don't know about?"

"Kane," Nathan was unfazed by the sudden outburst. "We are werewolves, or did you forget? I can detect her in you. She is in your mind. You swore off love after the- after Elvara..."

"Don't you dare mention her!" Kane snarled suddenly, this time taking the old man by surprise with his savage ferocity. "Do not dare mention her!"

"It is a reality you'll have to face sooner, perhaps even soonest," Nathan maintained his coolness. "This human you are with now- she is innocent. She knows nothing and is innocent in all this! If anything happens to her-"

"Nothing will." Kane swore- just as a scream rent the night air.

"If anyone wanted you dead, you'd be dead already," Nathan warned quietly as Kane started hurrying away. His voice carried with it a steely snarl. "Not all of us are out seeking your destruction Kane."

***

"Shhh! You'll wake up the others," the voice warned as a strong hand was clamped onto Samantha's mouth. "We don't want them awake while we talk."

Samantha tried to speak but the strong hand prevented her, and all she could do was squirm. Whoever it was whirled her around, but did not let go of her mouth. Through frightened eyes, Samantha saw dark eyes and gleaming white teeth behind very red lips. The rest of the face was covered. With paralyzing dread, Samantha realized she was face to face with a female werewolf. For the very first time since she could remember, Samantha experienced real terror.

"Where is he?" the shadowy figure seethed and uncovered Samantha's mouth. Her eyes shone darkly as if warning her not to scream again. The rest of her remained obscured by the dark cloak she wore, as well as the dark shadows they were in. Samantha opened her mouth, but no words came out.

"You know what he did, don't you?" The woman leaned closer, revealing part of her face. Samantha couldn't tear herself away from the hypnotic gaze of the dark eyes. Then, before Samantha could react, she felt her hand grabbed in a vice grip and was pulled to her feet. The two stood very close- despite the terror welling within her, Samantha noticed that the other woman was a foot shorter.

"Well?" the woman prompted with a snarl.

Samantha took two steps backwards and shook her head. Still she couldn't look away from those eyes searing and scorching into her very soul.

"You humans are foolish. Why do we bother with rules about not killing you? Your own fear rules you adequately."

"Please... what do you want?" Samantha heard herself croak. The other woman bowed her head a moment before answering. Samantha celebrated the release from the dark, hypnotic stare by drawing in relieved breaths.

"You have what is mine," the woman spoke softly. The voice was loaded with fury though, "Every night I stare and howl at the stars; asking for the aching void-" she thumped at her chest furiously, the sudden movement startling Samantha as evidenced by her loud gasp.

"In here," the other woman clutched at her cowl and tugged. "I've had him physically-" she paused and drew in a sharp breath, as if such a recollection was still fresh in her mind, and perhaps it was. She shuddered slightly then licked her lips. Sam envisioned a predator antagonizing its prey before devouring it. She was indeed the prey to this angry she wolf.

"But his heart, you have it. You, a mere human, have stolen-"

"Nothing! I have stolen nothing!" Samantha heard herself blurt out. She was shocked at the forcefulness of it. She felt slight elation rise within her as she watched the light fade from the other woman's dark eyes. Feeling emboldened, she took a step closer to the she wolf. The other did not move an inch.

"Careful of what you say next," she warned with a snarl. Samantha, who had opened her mouth, shut it, but did not move. The other woman raised her nose and sniffed the air.

"He's here. See, he can't stay away from you. He's blocked me, I can't read his thoughts, but I bet he's thinking about you, naked, aching with need, screaming for him, pulsating with desire..." she took a step closer, so close Samantha could feel her warm breath on her face. She started leaning even closer, till their faces nearly touched.

"Tell me," she crooned with a soft snarl and licked her lips. To Samantha's horror, she noticed her canines lengthening slowly. "Will you submit to him this cold night? Is that why you are prowling in the dark, looking for him?" Samantha felt a hairy hand touch her cheek. With all the force she could muster, she lifted her own hand and swung out. It was caught effortlessly and flung aside.

"Let's not be violent, please," the she wolf, whose canines were beginning to recede, snarled in placatory tones. "I would have an unfair advantage if we were to fight, wouldn't I?"

"No, you wouldn't," a deep voice suddenly broke in from the shadows. The she wolf turned suddenly and snarled. A deeper growl answered back, followed by the appearance what Samantha could only have described as a very large dog walking on two legs. She had seen him turn the previous night, but now he seemed larger, stronger, and more dominant that he was in his element and was not trying to suppress it. His eyes glowed crimson like live coals and a fury flamed within.

Samantha couldn't move. Frozen on the spot by paralyzing fear mingled morbidly with wonder, awe and shock, she could only watch as the she wolf, without much effort, suddenly transformed, and where just a moment ago stood a woman shorter than her now stood a beast a foot taller, snarling with as much ferocity as the other even huger beast that had materialized from the darkness.

Words she could understand, snarls she could not. When the two werewolves faced each other and started growling, Samantha fled. She had barely moved two steps when she bumped into another body- oh God, how many are they- she heard her mind wonder as her mouth opened to scream. She felt herself caught effortlessly, lifted easily and placed on a shoulder. The beast started moving very fast. Samantha could only thump at its back with her fists.

"Let me go!" she screamed. "Put me down!"

"Not until we're somewhere safe!" a deep voice answered her. Suddenly she felt so much relief wash over her, culminating in tears.

"Kane?" she sobbed. "Kane, is it you?"

"It's me Sam- it's no longer safe for me to stick around- but first I have to get you home."

"Put me down!" she demanded the moment she deduced they were out of the park. "I can walk."

"Stick close and do as I say." He set her down. It took a moment to orient herself, looking around them, she realized where they were; close to the place she had found him being torn to shreds by his own kind two days prior. They stopped for a moment and peered into the narrow alley, each with thoughts they did not share with the other.

Sighing deeply, he ran a hand through his hair, just as she resumed walking. *How could I have been so careless,* he wondered. *Damn this woman and her irresistible guiles.*

They walked a short distance, when suddenly, she stopped and grabbing his hand, pulled him towards a large tree near the end of the street they were on. Had it been any other time, he would have perhaps admired its nightly guiles of silhouetted leaves, chilly breezes and nocturnal creatures darting about.

But he couldn't at that moment, for he had seen her face. He was in more trouble with her than with Galou, it seemed. Once under it, she stopped and crossing her arms, glared up at him. He glared back at her, but not with as much ferocity.

"Well?" she prompted when he didn't seem to understand what she wanted.

"Well what?" he inquired innocently.

"Do I slap it out of you?" she fumed. "Speak, tell me I wasn't about to be mauled by your girlfriend."

"What?" he scoffed, then chuckled. She really itched to slap him. A hard hand across his face to wipe off that annoying indecisiveness. As if sensing what she was thinking, he took a step backward and thrust his hands into his pockets. Still, she waited.

"I can't tell you everything." His deep voice added to the night sounds quietly. "But if you are patient, I will in my own time."

"Kane," she stepped closer. "Danger seems to follow you. Your girlfriend wanted to tear me to pieces after accusing me-"

"Let's not talk about that!" he seethed suddenly, surprising her. "If you are patient, you will find out everything soon enough."

Kane felt trapped. Deep down he knew Esther and Nathan had been right. He shuddered when he recalled finding Galou with Samantha. If she hadn't screamed when she did, if he hadn't been around, if- if- he sighed suddenly. The 'ifs' were many, but at the moment, he realized he was thankful that he had happened to be there just on time.

Despite the angry frustration welling up in him, he had to agree, they had been right, and especially Esther. She had warned that Samantha would do anything once her mind was set; and now here they were, he having just rescued her from a demented werewolf.

Looking at her as she vented, he sensed that deep down she was glad, even elated, to see him. Her face and especially her eyes, despite the fury flashing in them, reflected an innate relief that he found deeply satisfying, despite his dilemma.

Samantha felt the anger welling like a thick liquid from deep with her. She released it in short breaths as she regarded the man standing quietly in front of her, placating her with monk-like calmness. He truly needed a slap. She realized she had already raised her hand to do it when a new noise alerted them both, breaking the unpleasant tension between them. They whirled around simultaneously, only to see something dark silhouetted as it flew away.

"An owl." They said it together, the relief evident in their voices.

"I don't have anything to say," He broke the silence that had descended, "But I'll make sure you're safe."

"Big words," Sam murmured under her breath. If he heard her, Kane did not make the slightest impression to show that he did. Silence returned and the two remained as they were without moving, each daring the other with their eyes to make any move, each trying to will the other out with their presence and each testing the other's resolve by remaining silent. A moment passed, and still neither made any move to break their gazes. Only their breaths broke the silence.

It was sudden, so sudden that everything around them was shocked into silence. They clashed- and their mouths met perfectly, as if they had been rehearsed for just that moment. They clawed at each other, as tongues sought furiously, exploring what words had failed to express; their innermost wants, wishes, yearnings. Everything else around them vanished, leaving them to the mercies of their own pent-up feelings.

Not until their bodies demanded that they needed air did they part to breathe. As if communicating wordlessly, they sought out each other's hand and set off. To where, none cared, as long as it was a place that would afford them the chance to let their bodies express as well as define what their kiss had started.

They were onto each other the moment the door was closed behind them, but something was different; the magic was gone, reason had returned, and with it logic, which at the moment demanded that they deal with the reality ruining such moments as those.

"Are we safe here?" She asked suddenly, looking around as if she had just realized that they were in her apartment.

"You are, I'm not." He crossed over to the couch. "That is why I must leave."

"Kane!" she gasped suddenly. Their moment earlier had not allowed her to think of such a prospect, but now, and the way he had said it made it painfully real. He would have to leave.

"Where will you go?" She joined him on the couch. He smiled briefly then took her hand. She brushed long strands away from his face as he regarded her with a gentle look.

"Samantha," He touched her cheek. "I have enjoyed my moments with you."

"Kane," she heard the fear and the dread in her own voice. "Is that all, moments with me?"

He took a moment, though he did not break his gaze. Slowly, he shook his head.

"Please," she sighed. "I want to hear you say it." She begged with her whole being.

"No."

She could have burst with elation as it built up deep within her- it took several deep breaths to contain it. The sparkle in her eye said so much though, and even more when she realized that he had more to say.

"I regret not a single moment with you, Samantha. Moments I would share over and over again. Were it not for the misfortune about to see us part, I would cherish your presence forever."

Samantha held his steady gaze as a rush of emotions welled up in her. Blinking fast to contain the tears, she drew in a deep breath, and smiled. She wanted her question to be expressed in the happiness she had just experienced at his words.

"Dare we hope Kane?" she rested her head on his shoulder. She wanted to feel his reply, and so she waited. She felt him draw in a deep breath and smiled. His silence had spoken even louder. The beautiful moment was ruined by a sudden shrill note, accompanied by impatient vibrations. Samantha rose with a sigh and crossed over to her desk. It was Avenue, and from a quick check, this was his hundredth call, if not more. Samantha picked the phone up and walked out of the room.

"It's Avenue," she whispered to Kane as she disappeared into the bedroom.

***

"I go to take a leak, I hear a scream, and when I get back, you were gone!" Avenue's angry voice came through the moment Samantha answered the call. "How many missed calls did you find on your phone?"

"Too many-" Samantha smiled. "My phone is warning of space shortage!"

"Seriously though, what happened? Who screamed? Why did you leave without waiting for me?"

"Ave- you said it, someone screamed. I wasn't going to wait and see who it was."

"Well, I called the police, as did others at the park. I promised I would call them once I found you-"

"You what?" Samantha shrilled into the phone. "You did what Ave?"

"Sam- your reaction raises a few questions. It's just the police, not the FBI!"

"Well-" Samantha changed the phone to the other ear. "I need a favor, Ave. I'm fine, I'm at home. Please don't trouble yourself calling them." There was silence at the other end, and Samantha thought he had hung up. She glanced at the screen- it was still connected. Presently, she heard rustling.

"Samantha Binds," she winced at the mention of her full names. "What is going on?"

"Well, nothing-" she paused as a flurry of ideas rushed through her head. "Ave, a moment please? I'll call you back-"

"No, you won't," he sounded resigned, and Samantha felt a stab of affection.

"I will, I promise." She drew in a deep breath, "I may need a favor from you."

"Well, I believe you now. Don't delay, Sam!"

"I promised, didn't I? Stay close!" With that she disconnected the call with a swipe and dropped the phone on the bed. She frowned, deep in thought. Kane had indicated he would have to leave. He hadn't said where, but if he could find a place to spend the night, then she would have a plan by morning.

As much as she wanted to spend the night with him, the danger was all too real- and he would not jeopardize her life further, she was sure. I'm not too keen on meeting that she-wolf again, she thought with a shudder.

Kane watched her hurry out of the room and felt thankful, for he needed a moment. So much was happening around him and to him, and yet, he felt he no control over any of it. Not even his growing feelings for the woman in whose apartment he now was. Sighing deeply, he sat back and closed his eyes. It was time he tried to express- but only to himself- some of what was happening, had happened and would most probably happen to him and around him.

Topmost- Nathan and Esther's urging that he return to Hale face the Council of Ethics and prove his innocence. He didn't have that evidence that he was not a killer. Then there was Galou. Kane felt his mouth sour at the thought of his former mate. He wasn't ready to think about her though, unless she represented real danger to Samantha.

Samantha, ah, now that was a name that brought a smile to his lips. She was another case. Whenever he found himself thinking about her, he found himself wishing he had met her in a different setting, not in the situation he was in then. It was futile to try and deny his feelings for her, and just a moment ago, he had expressed himself. He felt a sweet thrill course through him as he recalled how she had just reacted, and her follow-up question.

In another setting, sweet girl, he thought, *perhaps in another world where I am not running away from even my own life.*

He felt his mind take him back to an earlier time, when he had expressed himself the same way to another human. Back then, nothing had been chasing him, nothing had lurked in the shadows and decrepit cars waiting, ready to pounce.

In fact, he thought, he had been the one chasing life, realizing dreams, shaping a destiny for himself and Elvara- at the thought of the name, he opened his eyes suddenly and sat up. I'm not yet ready, he thought... Just at that moment, Samantha, reappeared, looking flushed and jovial, as if she had just figured a solution to all their problems.

"Kane, I may have a solution for tonight," she announced as she exited the bedroom and entered the living room. "I'll tell you while we eat."

It didn't take long to reheat the food she had prepared earlier during the day. As they ate, she elaborated on part of her plan and he objected, just as she had suspected. She persisted though and when eating was done, she rushed to the bedroom to call Avenue.

Kane rose and crossed over to the large window north. There was nothing to see this dark night, but he still peeped out as his mind whirled with questions, some unanswerable, some requiring more rumination before answers were attempted. The main concern were the words that had just passed between the two of them there on the couch. Expressions that coursed through him in deep thrills, but at the same time escaped him in worried sighs.

The woman was, well, unique, assertive, outspoken, short-fused at times but well intentioned if one viewed things from her point of view. He felt like a third observer standing close by, watching his whole being drawn in, giving in to something he had sworn off for life and with helpless abandon, realizing that he was enjoying every moment of it; Love. The word invaded his mind without warning, and he drew in an audible gasp. She had used the last word he would have expected her to, and his silence had answered her loudly and clear.

The last thing he wanted was to give her hope, the hope that her void he could fill. He couldn't. He would have wanted to, but he simply couldn't, not as he was, not in his present state of affairs.

As he stood by the window, Kane allowed his mind to express some of the thoughts he had locked away for so long. Topmost were the ideas he had espoused back in Hale, ideals that had been hijacked and modified to suit others' selfish reasons more than they had been initially meant to. Once everything had backfired and resulted in human deaths, he had been blamed... and had been hunted down. They had been ruthless, merciless, heartless. And a woman he had given hope had perished.

"Will you let him spend the night there, Ave, yes or no?" Samantha asked, exasperation begin to set in her voice.

"Then what follows?" Avenue's voice shrilled into her ear. "What did he bewitch you with?" Avenue could be obstinate at times.

"Stop asking so many questions!" she shrilled back irritably, then softened a little. After all, this was her friend and she needed his help. "Look, once all this is over I'll fill you in, promise!"

"Once *what* is over? Does it have anything to do with guilt and innocence? That is what I gathered from their whisperings with Esther-"

"I hate you so much right now!" Samantha fumed furiously, "I'll-"

"Fine! I'll host him for the night. I'll let you borrow my jeep in the morning, so that you two may escape to God knows where. I'll- what else, give my soul?"

"Thank you! Now come get him."

"Sam! I just agreed to-!" Samantha disconnected the call and returned to the living room.

"He's on his way- hey, dozed off already?" she startled him. He opened his eyes and rubbed them- after a hearty meal, Kane looked as if he would have preferred to drop there right where he was and sleep.

However, he made an effort to stay awake when she joined him at the couch. Even sleepy, his senses were still alert, and he smiled wryly when he noticed her rapidly glazing eyes feasting on him.

"If we try to, I'll never leave," he laughed. "I feel as you do too."

"Oh Kane, why is this happening?" she lamented. "Don't we have a right to happiness?"

He shrugged without saying anything. He stood up and walked to the middle of the room, where he held out his hands.

"We could be happy before your friend arrives. Care to join me?" She didn't need to be asked twice. She crashed into his arms like a young child after a considerable absence. Holding each other close, they started moving rhythmically, letting whatever song was in their minds dictate their moves.

Minds do reason, bodies do not. As they held each other and sought comfort through silent music, gazing into each other's eyes and communicating more than words could have, their bodies took over.

Suddenly, his lips looked too tempting not to kiss.

Suddenly, her cheek felt too good not to be caressed.

Neither mourned the loss of reason when slowly, tentatively, their lips met- at first brushing, trying each other out, before settling in for a languid kiss. Tongues made love as each explored the other's warm deliciousness.

"I feel so much love right now," she breathed.

"As I do," he breathed back.

"Let's make love for the rest of our lives!" She pulled him even closer, "Let's never stop!"

"Is it possible? I mean, is it possible to stop?" He welcomed her closeness with gentle but urgent thrusts of his hardness.

"What do you think?"

"With you by my side? No. It is not."

But a loud knock at the door *did* stop them. Giving up their heightened fervor to disappointment, she rushed over and after a quick peep, opened the door.

"Why do you even have a phone?" Avenue started the moment he was inside. It took but a moment to look at them both before understanding seemed to dawn on him. "Did I interrupt something?"

"We were just about to pack." Samantha avoided Avenue's suspicious scrutiny of them both, while Kane stood there, as if unsure of what to do or say next.

"I've decided I'll help your new friend," Avenue replied. "He can have my old room. Now, what can I do while you two recover from whatever it is that has both of you flushed?"

"Help us pack," Samantha pointed towards the bedroom. "Why don't you get started while I fill in Kane on the rest of the plan?"

Avenue smirked and left the room.

"There was more than your friend giving me a place to spend the night?" Kane frowned. "Up to this point you've done more than enough..." He took her hand. "Look, I'm sorry I got you into this Samantha, including your friend. Had I known..."

"Kane, I don't regret helping you," Her face brightened up. "I have the best idea though."

"What is it?" Kane asked, half afraid of the answer.

"My grandfather's cabin near the valley- don't worry it's nowhere near Hale. He used to live there during hunting seasons. My family inherited it. We can go-"

"No!" he blurted suddenly. "I'm not putting you in any more danger. It is bad enough as it is."

"Kane- I'm in danger as well," she looked up at him. "You saw the woman! Who knows-"

"She would never hurt you," Kane tried to reassure her, though Sam was shaking her head as he spoke. "She would never hurt a human."

"Kane, she already did. She hurt me with her words."

Suddenly, Kane's nostrils flared, and his eyes flashed.

"What did she tell you?"

"A lot. She said a lot of things. Words hurt too, you know, and hers cut like a sword."

"What did she say?" Kane demanded. Sam stepped away from him and seemed to be in deep thought.

"Well, I stole you from her, for one-" She counted it off her fingers. "You did something-"

"My God! She's spreading lies!" He seethed as he started pacing around. "She's making everything worse! Did she say anything else?"

"She-" Sam paused. "You know what? Let's help Avenue with the packing. We don't have a moment to lose. It's close to midnight already."

"Wait Samantha, what else did she say?" He followed her as she headed for the bedroom. He paused at the door just the same thought hit them both- her job. Avenue must have been thinking about the same thing too. He paused in stuffing stuff into a duffel bag to ask the question.

"M'lyka will hold for me," she assured the two men. "She's more than capable."

She answered him as she pulled out another duffel bag from the closet, then started selecting more clothes.

"How many of you are going?" Avenue asked when he noticed the second bag.

I'm not filling this one to capacity- Kane will need a few clothes before we leave."

"Doesn't that mean going into town? To a boutique?" Avenue glanced at Kane who took a moment to understand the implication. Samantha did not pause in her packing.

"It does," she started shoving shoes into the bag. She pointed at a spot on top of the closet and he looked. Understanding, he closed over with one step and picked up a pair of shoes then handed them to her. "Do we have a choice?" When she realized that both men were staring at her she straightened up.

"This is more than petty differences with my sister. So what, we don't get along, but this," she waved her hands, "is bigger."

Avenue just shrugged while Kane brightened with understanding. Sarah Binds, the woman who had sold him clothes was Samantha's sister. Had she known that he and Samantha were together, was that why she had been so friendly? It was a question with no immediate answer.

"Let's leave," Avenue picked one bag, Kane the other. The three walked into the living room.

"You'll join him in the morning?" Avenue paused and said it a way of confirmation rather than a question.

"Yes," Samantha glanced at Kane, "I'll come with my car and leave it there. We'll take your jeep." Avenue sighed deeply but said nothing. He opened the door and walked out. Samantha grabbed Kane's hand just as he was about to follow Avenue. She gazed at him-

"Not now, please?" Avenue interrupted them suddenly and rudely. "I have an early morning tomorrow-" He fished out his phone. "And tomorrow is less than an hour away. Please?" He stood aside as Kane passed. With a furious frown at Samantha, he followed him.

Chapter 9

When her phone startled her, she was already awake. It took a moment to realize that it was a call and not the alarm that had shrilled suddenly.

"Talk to your boyfriend!" Avenue's voice barked suddenly the moment Samantha picked up.

"You said the cabin is nowhere near Hale?" Kane's deep voice came through. Samantha felt a wave of relief wash over her suddenly.

"It is not," she assured him confidently. "And even if it was," she continued. "Would they have the audacity to follow you there?"

"Who knows?" He paused a moment. "Will you take long to get here?" he asked quietly.

"No," she assured him again. "Just getting a few things in order." She listened and heard the call disconnected. She slid out of bed and cursed loudly as she tripped on her way to the bathroom.

Back from her ablutions, she started preparing herself. Just then her phone buzzed, startling her slightly. She tapped at the screen, frowned at it, tapped it once more then replaced it back on the table.

Half an hour later, Samantha was sitting in M'lyka's cluttered kitchen, convincing her friend that her mind was working perfectly.

"Running off with that" M'lyka indicated with her hands, "werewolf, how is that not insanity?" Samantha said nothing. She gulped down her cocoa and rose.

"His name is Kane!" Sam blurted suddenly, taking her friend by surprise. She too was surprised by the sudden forcefulness with which the words left her mouth. She glanced at her friend. M'lyka was smiling snidely.

"He must be great, with you defending him like that. Will you keep him? What about Nelson?"

"Who is Nelson- oh that creep? He sent me a text this morning. Didn't read it though."

"Sam," M'lyka tried in a conciliatory tone, "you have a job, a career. You have friends, me and Avenue. You have family- well, you have us. What more could you want?"

Samantha started walking out, picking her way around paint cans and pieces of wood. M'lyka followed her, tripping on her own messy floor, while raising her voice with every word. "How do you know you'll be safe Sam?" she shrieked at her friend. "What makes you trust him so much that you lose your sense?"

"How is the painting going?" Samantha asked suddenly, catching her friend off guard. M'lyka seemed lost for a moment before recovering from her friend's impetuous question.

"We are not changing the subject!" she warned sternly. "I feel like drowning you in paint to bring back that sanity he's taken away!"

"I met another werewolf, last night," Samantha spoke without much feeling, her hand on the door. "She is in town. Probably," she added before walking out and hurrying to her car.

She glanced back. M'lyka had a weird look on her face as she regarded her friend, the news affecting her such that she remained rooted to the spot. Before she could recover, Samantha had started her car and sped off, laughing.

***

For the first time in years, Sam was about to go back to a place she had sworn to never set foot in. Her mind was about to recall what had brought about such a decision, but she overruled it by turning to Kane. She had driven to Esther's and without much fanfare and had left her car there, taking Avenue's jeep. It was a manual, but not a deterrent to her. She shifted confidently, her inputs resulting in the desired output, and they were off.

"I'm glad we decided to do this," she enthused and smiled at Kane as they exited the main road and took a dirt road. "It feels all so perfect."

"It should be sufficiently safe until I can think of what to do," he replied seriously. His grave mood did not affect her sunny one though as she continued smiling and also enjoyed a peace she had not experienced for a long time. The jeep reacted to her every input faithfully as she maneuvered expertly, avoiding holes as well as large stones that must have dislodged from the steep precipice on their right.

"It was great that Avenue gave us her jeep," she spoke again. "My car wouldn't have made it." He did not say anything but continued to look far ahead, seemingly in deep thought. Sam, still unfazed by his silence suddenly seemed to notice the radio and leaning over, turned it on. It happened that her favorite song started just at that moment. She bobbed her head and tapped the steering wheel in sync to the beat-

"Please turn it off," he spoke suddenly. Sam glanced at him with a slight frown, but did not make a move to turn off the music. Kane glanced back at her, then at the radio. For a moment, it seemed as if the radio was the source of whatever it was that was giving him such a foul mood.

Sam did not like the sinking feeling she experienced just then on realization that perhaps he was not as elated as she was about this trip, about had happened between them- perhaps not even her. Oh God, she thought with dread, he's not happy that I'm here. The sinking realization, once settled in the pit of her stomach was followed by one of disappointment. She opened her mouth- just as he opened his,

"Turn the darn thing off," he repeated, seething the words through clenched teeth. Feeling her own anger start to rise, Sam leaned over and pressed a button, increasing the volume. Kane glanced at her, dark eyes even darker, then jabbed his fingers into the radio buttons with abandon. His deed did not bring about the desired results. The radio did go off, and with it most of its face. Before, it had been an aesthetically pleasing array of LED screen and well-arranged buttons. Now the screen was cracked and the buttons buried deep inside and in no particular pattern. Sam turned to him, face aghast with disbelief.

"Kane, what have you done?"

"I just pressed it a little. It broke by itself," he defended himself.

"Why are you in such a foul mood?" she heard herself shout above the roar of the engine. "If you don't want my company you just say so!"

"Don't shout so much," she heard the soft snarl beneath his voice, which had taken on a steely edge. "You're proving to be too much."

"You are one thankless beast, you know that?" She felt hot tears form suddenly, threatening to spill.

"I am not a beast." He defended himself with a hint of feeling. "Perhaps you mean the night we spent together? Thank you."

"You're just like the rest," Samantha bristled just as the tears slid down her face. "Be gone as soon as possible. I don't ever want to see you again."

"Don't worry, you won't," he finally looked at her. His eyes had taken on a darker gleam and his canines showed when he snarled. Sam stared back at him with blazing eyes. "I'm not overly fond of humans-" He gave her a once-over sweep through narrow eyes. "Especially ones who demand thanks after throwing themselves at strangers."

Sam gasped and gawked at him in disbelief. She stomped on the brakes, bring the jeep to a screaming halt. She didn't press in the clutch to disengage the wheels from the engine, and it shuddered to a stop. Silence reigned for a moment before she turned, and with very calm and controlled movements pointed at the road.

She didn't need to say it. Without a word from him too, he opened the car's door and slid out. She did not look at him as she turned the ignition, disengaged, engaged, cursed when the engine spluttered to a stop, turned the ignition again, disengaged, engaged and with a sudden jolt, sped off, spewing dust and rocks behind her.

He was sitting at the front step when she pulled up at the cabin. Samantha stopped the jeep and looked at him long and hard. Her anger would not let her wonder how he had reached there before her, never mind finding the right place.

Despite her anger, she took a moment to scan the place she had not set foot for more than sixteen years. She marveled at how tall, large and thick some of the trees had become. The flowers bushes she had tended to as a child were now unattractively all over the place, including the wide path that led up to the cabin.

She looked at it and felt like crying again. Decrepit and sagging with neglect, it was in a sorry state, and sitting there choked by bushes and trees, it seemed to scream at her for rescue. I'm going to take care of this place from now on, she vowed silently, before turning to glare at Kane sourly.

"I thought I was too much," she spoke before he did. "So, what are you doing here?" Kane stood up. She observed him a moment and noticed the denim jeans he had on, and the checked shirt. On the steps where he had been sitting was a leather jacket. So Avenue had played dress-up with him, she thought as she felt a sudden stab of sour affection mingled with a sweet feeling of hatred.

He started towards her, then stopped when she took a few steps back. He help up his hands in surrender and attempted what he believed to be a reconciliatory smile.

"I could not leave just like that," he squinted as tufts of hair got into his eyes. They were no longer as dark as they had been earlier. He made no attempts to swipe the hair with his hands, which he held in front of him, as if bidding her to run into them. "I came to apologize before I leave."

"Well?" she prompted him. A sudden gust of wind intruded dustily, and she pulled her plaid jacket tighter around her.

"Well what?" He reacted innocently.

"You came to apologize, you said."

"I'm sorry Samantha." He sighed deeply, "There's so much going on in and around me, and- I guess I made the mistake of letting off some of the steam on you." He pointed at the jeep. "And your friend's radio." As if on cue, both took a single step towards each other.

Samantha felt her emotions begin to well up within her as she continued looking at him, standing there, tall, muscular, and arrogant, she thought.

"Look Kane, you used some hurtful words. I thought we had something- I dared to hope, I withstood your pride, but why in hell's sake would you say what you just did to me?" No longer able to hold it, she felt the tears come, hot with anger, but mostly disappointment.

"Please- Nothing, including your self-centered apology would make me forgive you. I'll deal with the pain."

"I suspected that." He sighed, and she saw the pain in his eyes. He took a step closer, but she did not. She did not step backwards though.

"Samantha Binds, I came back in the hope that even though I leave, nothing resembling bitterness remains between us. I would like to make you understand." Samantha crossed her arms and said nothing.

Another gust of wind passed between them, whipping his hair even more. To Samantha, it was one of those moments when a part of her wants things to be better, if not back to how they were before, while another part of her wanted to make him suffer, to have him feel tortured and tormented with regret for the rest of his life.

They remained quiet for a while, the tension between them seeking relief from the numerous nature noises about them in the overgrown bushes and on the trees. She wanted him to make her understand. She wanted him to apologize. She wanted him to take away the pain he had caused her, and yet, she wanted nothing to do with him, not even to hear his deep voice forming words that seemed to come from the Victorian era.

Due to this ambivalence on her part, Samantha remained quiet and waited, though she tapped her foot in impatience.

"In Hale," he started quietly. She did not look at him but rather focused her eyes on a small red and green bird that had found a fragrant bush nearby very interesting.

However, she couldn't turn away her ears, and his deep voice found its way in. "I was a medical research assistant. I met her while working there, but she was not local. We hit it off, though none of us took it seriously. One night when I was about to end my shift, she expressed interest-" Samantha glanced at him sideways, then resumed her observation of the small bird. Another one had joined the first one. Her mind screamed at him to continue.

"She- we had fallen in love. We couldn't hide it, but we couldn't stay apart either. It affected my output, but still, we saw each other. In an effort to refocus and take my mind off her, I took an interest in more than my job. In the course of my investigations on the research facility, I discovered something of concern, something highly unethical going on."

Go back to you and her, Samantha screamed at him silently, *tell me how she became the cruel beast who nearly mauled me at the park!*

"When it was discovered that I knew what was going on, I was summoned by some members of the board. They explained it all to me, and in my gullibility, I crossed over to their side. Their explanations were not the only reason I did it though. There was the unpleasant aspect of blackmail, since one of them accosted me later- before I had agreed with them- and threatened to expose my ongoing relationship if I did not join. I was young, I was naïve, and I was in love. I joined them and I got to spend as much time as I wanted with my love."

Samantha winced at those words, 'my love'. She gave him another sideway glance, then resumed her observation of her favorite couple, the two small birds who were now chasing each other all over the bush. She glanced at him again-just as he took another step towards her. Almost instinctively, she took one toward him too.

"Something happened with the unethical trials and five humans died. I was on shift that night, but I was not responsible for them. Unfortunately, my earlier foolishness in poking my nose everywhere did not help much, and convincing the Council Police that I was responsible was not hard. I fought back. I threatened to expose the entire facility. I had evidence, I claimed. In the throes of bitterness at the betrayal, I forgot that I was not endangering only my life-"

Samantha had not realized when she had uncrossed her arms or when she had begun paying rapt attention with her eyes too. Her two bird friends, seeing that their new friend was no longer interested in them flew away in disappointed chirps. Her whole body silently signified that he continue.

"In the same facility was my brother Jonah, and my uncle Luke. Thinking they would come to my aid, I ran to them, me and her. They promised, they promised Samantha... but when the questioning began they-" Samantha winced, with a sympathetic sigh, took a step closer. It was his turn to face away, as if turning his head would have erased the pain in his eyes. Suddenly, he turned to her. His eyes were painfully red-rimmed and his lips trembled. "She died- they killed her-" Samantha looked confused.

"But we met her at the park Kane! She was your mate, she said as much and you did too!"

He was shaking his head furiously, "No, no, no, you don't get it." He heaved suddenly. "Elvara was a human."

No words could have been adequate. Not even the comforting hand placed gently on his shoulder, or the consoling hug that followed. But Samantha did her best as she genuinely consoled him silently.

"I wasn't forcing you into anything- I'm sorry if it seemed to be that way. I took your dilemma for granted, just to fulfil my own selfish needs." They were still outside sitting on the steps, and it was Samantha who had just spoken. The jeep was still where she had parked it, and they had not offloaded their bags, for they were yet to enter the cabin.

"I wasn't a saint too, you know." Kane took her hand. "I thought my behavior would drive you away before anything happened or went too far. This morning I realized that it had happened and it was going faster than I could safely keep up with. I meant none of those words Samantha."

"Renew my hope Kane." She lay her head on his shoulder, "Even if you have to leave, give me something." He did. Drawing her closer, he descended on her waiting lips gently. She responded with a quiet hunger as she sought him with her tongue. He welcomed her and as they embraced tightly and communicated with the kiss, a moment descended around them, a moment that was etched into their very being, since they were one at the moment.

Samantha gasped; the rooms, though sturdy, were dusty. The furniture had sheets on them. It was on these sheets that much of the dust had rested, as well as on the walls. She walked into the first bedroom. It was the largest, and just like the other room, dust sheets had been placed on the bed, bedside table, closet and a desk that was against the wall.

There was a lot of work to do. Since Kane had promised to help her clean before leaving for Hale, Samantha had provided him with a slasher. As she removed the dusty covers, she heard him begin hacking away at overgrown bushes. They did not speak much as they worked. Still, each had time for their thoughts as they busied themselves with cutting, dusting and sweeping.

Samantha understood; if she prevented him from leaving, he would not find the respite he sought. If she let him go, then she would have to keep the hope they had shared alive, she would have to wait for him to find his healing.

Kane felt lighter as he hacked away at obstinate bushes. His earlier recalling of Hale and Elvara had released a piece of him and as he worked, he realized that his thinking was more clearer, that he could at least let his mind express itself, even if to him. There was much he was yet to release, things that he was not yet ready to face.

He felt that to deal with that, he would have to go back to Hale. He had indicated to Samantha that she could hope, though deep down he felt apprehensive. He could fight for his innocence, that he was sure, but would centuries-old rules be changed because of the two of them? Was he willing to risk it and stick with her despite these age-old rules? There was much Kane wasn't sure about, but one thing stuck to him- in Samantha was the happiness he had sometimes recalled with nostalgic sighs.

He would fight to protect the hope he had planted, even if with his life. The day aged and with it, a common resolve that united the two, Human and werewolf. It did not need words as they took a break from their work and sought each other. His gaze as she had reappeared from the house all dusty, and as she had gazed back at him all sweaty was enough. Their kiss announced to their bodies that there was more to follow. He led her to the side of the cabin where soft grass had reclaimed and layered itself like a natural carpet.

They sat and resumed the kiss. He didn't have much to shed since he had taken off his shirt while working.

She ran her hands all over his wide chest as he lay on his back, groaning with tortured pleasure. She felt his hand slide up her tank top and rest on her stomach. She held her breath and felt it slide up till it found her breasts, covered from his teasing fingers. The hand slid around her and found the strap. A quiet click and she was free. His fingers found her breasts again. This time, she couldn't help drawing in a sharp breath as his fingers found her hardening nipples and started playing with them. She arched her back and abandoning his chest, pressed her breasts together as his fingers teased by tugging and squeezing gently.

She took off her top and lay beside him. She heard him groan softly when he noticed her eyes on his groin. Slowly, relishing every moment, she rubbed the hardness within and sighed with pleasure at his groans as he started grinding against her hand. His own was back on her now exposed breasts and he resumed his own teasing.

Slowly, she unzipped him and slid her hand inside. He buckled suddenly when her soft hand found his hard shaft. He twisted in sweet agony as she freed his nodding need, now at the mercy of her hands. He gyrated, grabbed her waist, squeezed her breasts and still she did not cease. She wasn't done, and his begging groans weren't enough to stop her. He had felt delicious coolness when freed, but now he felt himself slide into a warm wetness as she took him in her mouth.

A hand placed on his chest restrained him as she drove him mad with yearning, sucking and licking him expertly, teasing him whenever he reached the precipice, but not letting him cross over to relief land. She was busy torturing him, she didn't know when he had unbuttoned her pants, but suddenly, his hand was inside, testing her wetness, squeezing her sweet spot and rubbing her engorged lips.

She was too weak with giddy pleasure when he pulled himself away from her mouth and sat up. She gazed up at him through glazed eyes as he pulled off her pants. She felt the cool wind breeze curiously between her legs; and welcomed it with tingling pleasure, before his mouth invaded her and his tongue dove into her deepest desire, to taunt her into helplessness as she writhed and moaned in agony. His tongue found a waiting sweetness while his fingers squeezed her nipples to scream land.

She had tortured him, now he was on a revenge mission, of his own. Grabbing his hair, she moaned and thrust herself into his face, but it wasn't enough; she wanted more.

"Release me!" she heard herself moan weakly.

"Never!" She felt his breath drive into her warmly with his cruel reply. She sighed with emptiness when the warm mouth withdrew, but not for long. She anticipated it, believing herself ready. She wasn't. When he invaded, she screamed with pleasured agony. Surely he was bigger, longer? She didn't know and she didn't open her eyes to find out. As she received, she could only rise to meet his massiveness with determined thrusts of her own.

He drove mercilessly, not giving her a chance to fully express the moans that escaped her. One moan after another left her slightly parted mouth while her eyes remained closed. Still, he rammed, and did not stop until, sighting the shores of relief land, he slowed down to wait for her. Then, he picked up tempo again, diving deep into her desires, while she wrapped around him with pulsating wetness.

The explosive moment to cross over came; minds fled, bodies shuddered with electrifying intensity and unrestrained cries, which were picked up all around them by a sudden breeze to be celebrated far and wide. It took a moment to calm down and they remained as they were, joined in mind, body and purpose. Hope had been renewed.

"Are you afraid of anything, Kane?" She asked softly. He looked up and sighed. Evening had descended. They were in bed in the main bedroom, having just renewed their hope once again. Her head rested on his chest, and she could feel him draw in deep breaths. He was trying to contain his emotions, she knew. But she wanted to push him further, to test him, to see how much in control he was. The lovemaking was phenomenal, she admitted, amazing even. She still found it hard to believe that for once in her life, she could admit, at least to herself, that this felt real and wholesome too.

She lifted her head and looked up and into his face. His eyes had a faraway look. She rested her head on his chest once again and closed her eyes. Outside, an owl hooted to welcome the rapidly approaching night.

"Why do you ask that?"

"Curiosity, I think."

"If I tell you a bit, will it be enough?"

"Yes," she promised softly. He rose and sat on the bed, then stood up and walked over to the window. No longer was he overly self-conscious of his nakedness. He looked outside, as if afraid someone else might be listening, and would hear what he was about to divulge. From his sighing, it was evident that it was not something good.

"Long ago," He did not look at her. Sam remained where she was, eyes on his back, ears strained to catch his every word, "I watched someone boil to death. Don't ask who, don't ask where, and don't ask me anything. The sight of the boiling liquid, the hot steam-" he stopped suddenly and sighed even harder. "To this day I cannot stand hot liquids."

Samantha did as he bid and did not say anything. Her phone broke the silence. It was M'lyka. With a sigh, Samantha connected the call.

"You ran off and left me to deal with your mess!" M'lyka's voice shrilled into her ear.

"Why, what's wrong?" Samantha sat up straighter. Kane was still at the window, looking out.

"Nelson is looking for you! Mr. Reagan is willing to renegotiate, but he asked specifically for you!"

"Well, to hell with Nelson, you can tell him that, and as for Reagan, well, I lost interest." Sam uncovered herself and got out of bed, phone still pressed to her ear.

"If he persists?" M'lyka insisted.

"Part of the job does not involve between the sheets deals." Samantha sighed. "I know I may have led him on, but... tell him I'm out of the country. Anything else?"

"Yes. I found the she wolf!" The call was disconnected from the other end. Samantha dressed, as did Kane. Suddenly, he turned to her.

"We never took that walk." He gave her his hand and smiled. She smiled back at the memory of that day. Hand in hand, they walked out into the moonlight.

"There's nowhere to walk to." She looked around them.

"We can still sit outside." He indicated at a spot beyond the parked jeep. "Over there."

She let him lead her to the secluded spot, where they found a large boulder sticking out of the ground. Nearby was a large tulip tree. Samantha felt a sudden rush of thrill as they walked hand in hand and sat on it. Why anyone would want to ruin such moments as they were sharing was beyond belief.

So far Kane had enjoyed himself more than he could have thought possible. Even now as they sat leisurely under the moonlight, he relished holding her close, feeling her soft body pliant and responsive to his own firm one. On that rock, under the moonlight, he could sense her hazel eyes on him- he felt her move closer, and he held her tighter.

"Kane," she called him softly. She saw him turn towards her, though he did not answer.

"What happened to between you and Galou-why does she harbor so much hate?"

She moved closer. He could smell her scent as the breeze wafted across, around and about them.

"Wolf business, nothing to burden a human with." His voice was terse.

"Am I to feel safe with you while still in the dark about her?" She stood up. Kane did not move, but looked up at her, and through his dark eyes, she saw the conflict within. It startled her. He drew in a deep breath, "Yes, feel safe and ask no more." He patted the spot she had just vacated. Without a word, she rejoined him.

Around them, the bats flew silently. The crickets held their concerts noisily. The night breeze whooshed by, the waving trees and bushes announcing it with rustling leaves. High above them, the gibbous moon made numerous efforts to peep at the scene below; from the way she kept reappearing after eluding dark clouds which were chasing her. The tulip tree shielding them made sure that they had some privacy though, for they were in no hurry. In silence their minds sought meaning and understanding.

But hunger wouldn't let them. They returned to the cabin where she reheated the food they had brought with them. Despite the condition the place was in, the gas stove, once cleaned worked well, but that is after Samantha had checked for leaks with a hand-held meter. The same gas also provided the light that now guided them as they dug into delicious lamb chops dipped in thick gravy.

"It is suddenly so quiet," she observed suddenly. "I never liked this place to tell you the truth."

"Really?" He seemed surprised at her confession, "I find it peaceful and quiet."

"Frankly, I'd rather be in a noisy, smelly city, than in a quiet, boring countryside."

"What could be so boring about the natural?" he asked. "You can't hunt in a city."

"Why would I need to hunt?" she gave him a quizzical look.

"For food, sustenance. Why else... oh, I forgot, humans don't hunt."

"Damn right. We value life." She stripped a bone and chewed delicately.

"As is well evidenced by how you dig into those lamb chops."

"These?" She pointed with her fork. "Are store bought."

"Didn't they come from a lamb?" He peered at her.

"Not my concern. I don't burden my mind with where they came from..."

"You are okay with believing they are from the store, and that is that?" She nodded twice then pointed her fork at his face.

"Promise you won't go hunting while around here."

"Why not?"

"I'm uncomfortable with the thought," she shuddered.

"Okay. I'll get deer from the store." He smiled, then laughed at the look on her face.

"You're mocking me." She shook her fork accusingly. "But think of the local authorities sniffing around after finding gutted carcasses of deer all over. You ready to deal with whatever follows?"

"Samantha, what makes you think I'd leave deer carcasses all over, and gutted at that?" He sounded genuinely hurt at her insinuation. "Is that what you imagine we do, kill uncontrollably and leaving the mess behind?"

"That is what I heard. Isn't that one of the reason Leeve Valley divides the two societies? To protect humans from the savagery?"

"We're not like that." He sounded truly hurt. "We may be werewolves, but we are more civilized than your human minds could ever begin to fathom. Certainly more cultured than you humans; we don't need enforcement of morals by rule of law."

"What is that supposed to mean?" She stopped eating and looked at him.

"We are the superior species. The Leeve Valley protects our high culture from your degraded morals."

"You realize you're talking to a human?" It was her turn to sound hurt. "Do you hear yourself, the blatancy and the nerve to spew such- such assertions?"

"Spare me the correctness, human." His eyes turned a shade darker, "How are my opinions and views different from yours? Didn't you call us savages?"

"And you countered that by inferring to us as inferior?" She retorted back hotly.

"Aren't you?" His voice rose an octave.

"No! The nerve!" She glared at him. "No wonder we're kept separate!" She rose suddenly, upsetting the table and spilling some of the stew. She gave him one furious glance and stormed off.

She heard him enter into the bedroom. She was lying on the bed, phone in hand. She didn't turn around, even when she heard him approach.

"I came for a sheet. There are mosquitoes out there." When she made no comment, he continued, "The jeep is sufficient. I'll spend the night there."

She remained in stony silence as he fumbled around, perhaps looking for a sheet. Then, he left the room, but not for long. Without saying anything, he picked up one of the duffel bags that had contained a few items courtesy of Avenue. Samantha turned and without a word walked out of the bedroom. In a moment she was back, and what she saw him doing stopped her in her tracks.

He was packing. She stood there and felt the tears rise hotly, and still she said nothing. This wasn't how she had envisioned their parting. She wasn't going to break the silence though. Neither was he apparently, for when he looked up and saw her, he did not pause, nor slow down. He continued stuffing the few clothes he had into the duffel bag. On the small table was a glass wolf.

Samantha felt her mind decide to focus on it. She had gifted him with it after their lovemaking. If he took it, would it mean she meant something to him- that all that had happened between them mattered. What if he didn't take it? Would that signify the end of what she had admitted was the best time of her life? She drew in a deep breath, crossed her arms tighter, blinked away threatening tears and waited.

He was done packing; all the clothes that they had placed in the closet were gone, stuffed inside his duffel bag. He straightened up and looked about him. She waited. He was looking at the glass wolf. She watched his face closely, then his hand as he stretched it out- and placed it on his head to scratch it as if in deep thought.

Just leave it, it meant nothing! She screamed in her head while the frustration contorted her facial features. *It was all nothing! Nothing! Leave me... wait..!*

He was looking at the wolf. She held her breath as he leaned forward slightly, still looking at the wolf closely. She watched his hand- and two things happened at once. She saw a movement in her peripheral, and at the same time, she noticed him stiffen suddenly as he lifted his nose into the air.

"Sam!"

"Kane!" Both of them screamed at the same time as the walls rocked violently and sounds of wood splintering could be heard. In a moment, the small room seemed to be filled with large dogs. There was a blurry flurry of quick movements, painful screams, angry growls, hoarse shouts, pitiful cries and dull thuds. Sam felt herself falling... and blacked out before she could hit the floor. Her last image was that of Kane rushing towards her, terror written all over his face.

Chapter 10

When she came to, she was alone. The cabin was a wreck. Kane was gone. Even the bag he had packed was gone, as well as the glass wolf. She crawled shakily over to the bed and pulled herself up to sit on it. Her head throbbed furiously and her hands trembled uncontrollably.

She checked herself carefully for injuries and finding none, stood up on unsteady legs to takes stock of what could have happened by looking. She gasped when she saw blood on the floor and some on the walls.

Lots of it, it seemed to her.

Could they have taken him, she wondered. Or... she shuddered violently at the thought- *killed* him? She stifled a sob as she staggered out of the bedroom to see what other damage there was. Perhaps he was still around, too injured to move or cry for help, but still alive. Hopefully.

"Kane?" She whispered as she rounded the narrow hallway. The walls had deep claw marks on them. The wooden floor was all muddy, as well as damaged. In places, the wood was broken through. Through one particularly large hole on the wall she could catch glimpses of the moonlight as it peeked in tentatively.

"Kane?" She tried again, a bit more loudly this time. Save for the howling wind outside accompanied by noisy crickets, all was silent.

No Kane answered her. Sam slid to the muddy floor, wept then bawled her heart and feelings out, screaming his name over and over again. No one answered. Not even when the crickets quieted down, perhaps to accord her the required silence in case her lover answered, no matter how weakly, and she couldn't have heard otherwise. Still, there was no answer. Kane was gone. And Sam cried, for she was alone.

***

His foot slid across the incline. He threw out his hand and grabbed the first thing his fingers came into contact with, a small tree jutting off the precipice. Grabbing hold of the small tree with all the strength he could muster, he used it to regain his balance. He paused for a moment to catch his breath. Below him was the Leeve Valley, dark and full of uncertainties. Beyond it was Hale.

From where he was he was able to tune in and catch bits and snatches of conversations in the city, and it was no different from the noises that define a human city. Above him and over the valley was Green Bay, as was Sam. Sam. The thought jolted him into the present and he resumed his painful ascent. Suddenly, he sniffed the air. They were not far behind. Growling with determination, Kane covered the remaining gap and suddenly, he was on top of the valley.

Feeling faint with fatigue, he sank to the dusty ground and drew in sharp breaths. He had lost them, but just. Soon they would pick up his scent and would be hot on his heels again. He checked his wounds; a gash on his right side and a cut on his right leg. The injuries looked serious, but if he could get a moment to relax, then he would be able to heal. But at the moment, he couldn't even turn with such injuries. His strength was too low.

Suddenly he realized he had never really thought about the five humans he had been accused of killing.

While being dragged through the forest, injured and bleeding, he had caught most of what they had said, despite his state. It was obvious that his escape had created a buzz in

Hale, perhaps even an investigation. Indeed, something had happened for why else were they so keen on killing him?

If the city was still out for him, he would have been found by the ethics police. But the two of them, his brother Jonah and his uncle Luke, seemed determined to finish him off. If true; if evidence had been found proving his innocence, then Kane had a reason to survive, to fight and to defend his right to enjoy it. On the other hand, if the investigators had found evidence implicating him, they wouldn't have sent assassins after him, rather would the Council of Ethics have declared him a rogue. At the moment, he was just a fugitive.

This reasoning gave him hope. As he limped away from the valley and into the forest, Kane thought about how it had reached this point. He had discovered that the research facility in Hale had been researching into turned humans.

Kane had always been an advocate of turning willing adult humans then training them on how to control their newly acquired powers, but he had not for one moment imagined such an idea would be utilized to turn them and then subject them to cruel treatments in the effort of finding cures as well as solutions to all that rendered a werewolf mortal; notably, their susceptibility to silver. Human after human had been turned and then subjected to unimaginable torture, and Kane had looked the other way.

In his mind he had envisioned immortality for him and his love Elvara. However, she had died and he had lost his very freedom. Now they were after his life. He was still limping when he happened upon a cave over which trickled a very small waterfall. He drank greedily and after washing away some of the blood, he crept inside the cave, instincts alert.

His thoughts shifted to Samantha as he tried to settle and relax. Thinking about her made his head, side and leg pulsate with pain. Drawing in deep breaths, he closed his mind to all thoughts and focused on his battered body.

It was not howling, screeching, screaming or bellowing wild animals or buzzing and stinging insects that drove him out of the cave. He opened his eyes and realized he had fallen asleep- it was morning. His mind was full of thoughts of Samantha.

Neither was it the biting cold that had him staggering out. The sun, after a night's respite, dared to show its face; it was warm at first as it attempted to make amends with its heat onto a cold and chilly world that it had abandoned the previous day.

It was hunger that drew him out, cold and shivering. Crawling to a nearby rock, he sat facing the east. With as much effort as he could muster, he ejected all other thoughts from his mind and replaced them with all the aches and dullness in his mostly healed injuries.

True, more than his body yearned for healing, but of what significance was it if he consoled himself concerning Samantha but neglected his injured body? Wasn't it better if he got better physically and then deal with the emotional turmoil later? With this philosophy in mind, Kane refocused all his mental energy into his physical pains.

It proved a hard task for he was still chilled to the bone, and the sun, despite its best efforts, seemed a bit tardy in its timeless task of spreading its warmth. It didn't take long though… and Kane's patience started paying off. He felt the pain receding from his leg as well as his side, and when he opened his eyes, he watched as the ugly bruise on his exposed ankle started to fade.

It seemed as if an invisible eraser was passing over it. In a moment, nothing remained to show that there had been a gaping wound on his leg, not even a scar. He touched his side, then lifted what remained of his shirt and used his fingers to feel the flesh beneath. There was no gaping wound.

If only it was this easy to deal with the emotional scars that roiled like a demented storm in his mind! Why had he allowed his feelings and troubles to be part of his tryst with that human woman? What was it about her that made his heart hammer in his chest every time his mind brought into his consciousness her beautiful face, her soft shoulders, her sawing hips as they had walked. He had watched her... her hands on his skin, her soft sighs as she expressed her erotic desires with motion and emotion...

He groaned loudly when he realized the effects his mental images were having on his now rejuvenated body. No longer weakened with the loss of blood and crippling pain, Kane felt a strong urge to release all the pent up energy, and since Samantha was not here- where is she? He heard a small voice in his head wonder- the next thing that could satisfy him was food.

Standing up, he drew in deep breaths- and transformed, relishing every creak and pop as his bones realigned and changed. It didn't take long, but the experience left him feeling powerful, infinite, as if his human form had been a limitation, a hindrance to his full potential. And indeed it had been, for now, as he stood there, tall, strong and formidable, the werewolf could sense what the human had been unable to; food and in close proximity.

Lifting up his nose, Kane the werewolf let out a howl, utilizing every vocal chord in his throat. It was a call, a cry, a proclamation and a challenge. Once done, he remained as he was and waited. A strong breeze took up his howl and rushed off to deliver it. Nothing answered back, not even the birds which had been celebrating the morning sun. In a moment, the breeze was back, bringing with it all the noises of the forest, and the message that his proclamation had been heard. With a satisfied sigh, Kane bounded off to hunt, his instincts drawn by the inviting calls of deer grazing nearby.

He could not recall the path that they had used the previous evening when they had dragged him, injured and unconscious. The mere thought made him snarl softly. It wasn't his own person that he was overly concerned about though; he still had to find Samantha and... and then what? Suddenly, the possibility that perhaps what had happened to them the previous night was too much of a traumatic experience for her hit him hard.

It hit him with such force that he paused where he was and with a deflated sigh, allowed the possibility to have free reign in his mind. She wouldn't want anything to do with him. She was much too traumatized and had gone back to her family (had she even mentioned them to him except Sarah, the boutique lady?) She was lying in a hospital somewhere, injured, her mind gone (would she ever remember him and their nights of passion?)

Or, she was- he tried to deny the possibility, but the word forced itself into his mind- dead. Perhaps she had died. Try as he might, he couldn't push away the thought from his mind. Resuming his aimless sauntering Kane tried to recall the very last moments before Jonah his blood brother had knocked him out.

He had seen Samantha, scared and terrified but unhurt, screaming his name while one of the werewolves had restrained her. It had been Galou, he thought venomously. Then, just before blacking out, the very clear image of her extricating herself- or did that vile Galou let go of her? -her rushing towards Kane as he fell.

That was the last thing he could recall. Holding onto the last image firmly as evidence that she had perhaps survived the attack, Kane reoriented himself with the surroundings and finding a trodden path, he took it.

A short walk later he found it branched into several footpaths. Up to that moment, he still wasn't sure of where he was. Also, he was yet to pick up any scent that was not part of the natural surroundings about him. He paused for a moment and looked about him.

Of the clothing that had been on him, only his denim jean pants remained, and they were torn. Through the pants' tears bulged muscles that bunched with every motion as he turned about and sniffed the air. Only the wind, unaccompanied by any foreign scents answered his sniffs.

Clenching his fists, Kane abandoned all attempts at relying on his wolf instincts and decided to trust his reasoning. He observed the paths about him and decided on the one that seemed well-used. With decision firmly made, Kane Limaric started walking resolutely.

He must have walked for long, for soon he found himself in the deepest of the forest. Different sounds from the ones he had woken up to in the morning filled the tree canopies, echoing all over nature's ceiling of treetops.

He leaned against a nearby tree to try and still his screaming thirst. Since he had decided to reason rather than follow instincts, he realized that fruits would serve just as well as water in quenching his thirst. With this thought, he began searching the bushes as well as the trees for edibles. He didn't have to search for long.

Coming upon a highly fragrant bush, he recognized it and whooped in joy at what it held; a whole shrub filled with cape gooseberries, from immature green ones to the ripest, a succulent deep orange. He wasted no time and quickly knelt in front of the plants. He salivated as he tore open the soft calyx with trembling fingers and snipped the fruits off with his teeth.

Kane walked on, for how long he wasn't sure. He had loitered in the forest, he wasn't aware that he had walked into the valley. Presently, he came upon a dirt road. It took a moment to reorient his bearings, and when he did, he took and easterly direction. He didn't have to walk for long when he saw a homestead in a vast compound.

At the same moment, his nose picked up a scent that had him snarling softly. His brother and Uncle were close. Suddenly, Kane realized that he was tired of fighting, as well as something else- if he perished in their hands- or paws- there was the high likelihood that Samantha would be killed too. They had killed Elvara, they wouldn't hesitate to kill his new love too.

However, he reasoned, there was perhaps a way to save her. It required a huge sacrifice, but he wasn't ready to see another innocent person lose their life on account of him. With this new decision firmly set in his mind and evidenced by his clenched fists, he sat where he was and waited for his family.

***

The jeep obeyed Samantha faithfully as she maneuvered it carefully on the rough road. She was yet to see any other car. Having left the cabin very early and with the single thought of Kane torturing her mind, she had taken the jeep and driven. Her destination, Hale. She was still in the valley, and the city was on her right, beyond a ridge. So far the vehicle had made all the expected sounds.

But suddenly, it seemed to change its mind, with a knocking sound accompanied by smoke. Samantha sighed, then beat at the steering wheel in fury. *I thought this only happens in movies!* She screamed in her mind as she got out and looked both ways. Far off in the distance the way she had come, dust rose. Samantha leaned against the jeep to wait. Perhaps it was another car.

It was. As it drew close, Samantha stepped into the road and waved. She needn't have- the other driver was already signaling a she slowed and came to a stop behind the jeep.

"Thank God- it just died and-" Samantha rushed over and started speaking without pause.

"Don't worry, it happens." The other car's occupant, a woman, stepped out and approached Samantha with a reassuring smile,

"I can give you a lift- I'm going to Hale. Oh, leave it," she had noticed Samantha looking at the jeep worriedly, "No one will touch it. However, we can arrange for it to be towed once we arrive in Hale."

"Don't you have a number we can call?" Samantha fished out her phone through the car's window. The other woman shook her head, "Look around us. We are in a valley. Poor reception. Come, let's go."

Samantha got into the other car- she was the only other occupant besides the woman- and after settling in the passenger seat, closed her eyes.

I'm coming, Kane, she voiced in her head, *I'm on my way.*

When she opened her eyes, they were pulling into a driveway. It was lined with bougainvillea on both sides and in front of them was a large house, almost like a ranch house, Samantha thought as she exited. The other woman smiled encouragingly and beckoned,

"You seem tired. Perhaps a breakfast will rejuvenate you. Come! This house belongs to my friend. We will rest a while, try calling using their phone and then be on our way to Hale."

Indeed the woman had been right, in Samantha's opinion. The house did have an occupant, an elderly man who walked with a slight stoop, and the breakfast did her good, too. Now remained the matter of the phone call, and she requested as much, and as politely as possible. The other woman stood and beckoned, "It is in the study. Come." Samantha hesitated. Her sixth sense was beginning to kick in.

"Would you rather I called then?" The woman, noticing that Samantha was not inclined to follow her, smiled widely.

"Yes please. I'll wait here." The woman left the room just as a vehicle sounded outside. In a moment she was back, and Samantha noticed something akin to panic in her blue-green eyes.

"Karen sent you?" she whispered urgently.

"Um, no," Samantha looked confused as she shook her head, then replied hesitantly, "I'm looking for..." before she could say more, the woman grabbed her hand.

"Quick! You shouldn't be seen!" She whispered hoarsely as she pulled her. Samantha was even confused.

Feeling panic rise within her like bitter bile, she opened her mouth, but the other woman shushed her loudly.

"Shhh! This is for your safety!"

Samantha was unconvinced. Who was this woman, who was the stooped man who had served them and what was happening?

The woman pulled Samantha, now paralyzed into silence by terror into another room. She did not let go of her as she removed a cloak from the wall. Samantha shook her head dazedly when it was thrust at her.

"This is to protect you!" The woman whispered hoarsely, "Didn't Karen warn you?"

Samantha could only shake her head mutely.

"Damn her, sending you humans to me without going through the terms first. Did you swear before the Nog?"

Real fear was now blatant on Samantha's face. *Humans*, the woman had said. Suddenly she saw in her mind Galou at the park, threatening, imposing, spewing venom.

Samantha felt faint and the room spun around her. The other woman peered at her closely. A myriad of emotions and indecisiveness seemed to cloud her green-blue eyes momentarily, before her face cleared and she pulled Samantha even closer.

"Swear?" she shook Samantha as if the action would have made her understand what she was whispering about, or what was going on. Voices could be heard in the other room. "Did you swear before the Nog? This is your last chance!" The woman seemed frantic. "Answer me!"

"Lady, I don't know..." Suddenly the other woman shoved her roughly and before Samantha could voice her protest, a hand was clamped onto her mouth.

"Shhh!" the other woman shushed hoarsely, just as a shadow approached as they watched, and a figure passed by the narrow entrance without glancing their way.

Sam squirmed, but the other woman held her tighter with a superhuman strength. She couldn't have dislodged herself... and slowly, agonizing reality dawned on her that this was another werewolf, as she continued to struggle futilely, an idea, crude and hazy at first, began to form in her mind. Lessening her struggling from the vice grip, Sam tried to form rational thoughts, as well as make sense of what was going on.

"Karen wasn't there when I... ahem! ...when I came. No one said about swearing before Nod- Don- I mean Nog..!" she tried desperately.

"This is what happened last time!" To Sam's surprise, the other woman let go of her as she sighed in resignation, "Changing your mind the last moment... what did you think you were getting, ice cream?"

It was apparent that her opinion of Samantha was now contempt at what she perceived to be cowardice on Samantha's part in refusing to 'swear before Nog', whatever that meant.

"What- happens- now?" she asked in a shaky voice.

"We play our part and hopefully everything plays out fine," the other woman peered out. "And that means moving. Come!" she beckoned. The moment her back was turned, Samantha shoved her with all her might and fled the room. She heard the surprised snarl behind her as she crashed into the main room. Through her terror she glanced at the two men who had walked in- and froze. One of them was Kane.

Samantha stood rooted to the spot, wondering if perhaps she had gone mad, when she noticed both men glance behind her in alarm. Instinctively, she ducked, but not fast enough. She felt herself whisked up easily, strong hands wrapped around her waist.

"Oh, look," a familiar voice crooned in her ear. "It is the lover to my former lover." Samantha blacked out.

When she came to, she was lying on a bed. Someone else was in the room, standing by the window and looking out. Thinking it was the hateful Galou, Samantha scrambled up- the figure turned- it was Kane. Samantha grabbed her head and groaned. She was indeed mad.

"You are free to leave once you feel better." He spoke without looking at her, and his deep voice reminded her the first time she had heard him speak; emotionless and devoid of feeling.

"What is going on, Kane?" she whispered. She slid out of bed and stepped towards him when he did not reply. Suddenly, he whirled and faced her, his canines long. "I said you were free to leave," he snarled. "The jeep is all ready and waiting outside."

Sam could only stare at him with frightened eyes that were quickly welling up with tears. Hot tears that represented what she had endured in the last few days. Angry tears that despite what was happening in front of her, in her mind memories of the cabin and the shared moments were still fresh. Frustrated tears that whenever something perfect happened to come your way, behind it was something to sour up the experience. She had survived Galou, and twice, it seemed. She had proven she wasn't afraid of him. She had risked her life, her friends and her job. Hope had propelled her on, it had shown her to see beyond the immediate horizon, and as she stood there looking at the snarling man, she realized; and she acted on this realization.

Taking a step closer, she maintained eye contact as he snarled threateningly.

Deep within those red orbs of fury was her Kane. The beast's snarling did not deter her, and she approached till she was standing very close, so close she could, with faint but flaring hope, see behind the red eyes and hold onto it.

"Kane," she held out her hand. He did not move and he did not stop snarling. "I know you are in there, cowering behind this false exterior. I have seen the real you, and it is not the beast standing in front of me. I am not afraid of you. I never was. I can see the storm in your eyes, the turmoil, the torture, the suppressed trauma. You have let it consume you..."

She did not break eye contact. Not even when there was sudden commotion somewhere about them. The beast growled and tried to move, but she would not let it. She moved even closer to where it stood by the window. Her eyes probed into the dark storms on its face, invaded into the mind within, and there she stayed put. She would not move even when it lifted huge paws and landed them heavily on her shoulders.

Still she held despite the searing pain that travelled down her shoulder blades. Not even the fight going on outside could have torn her away from it.

"Leave!" the beast snarled ferociously, "You are free to leave!"

She shook her head determinedly. "I saw you," she whispered into the mind she was focused on, "I loved you, and I haven't stopped." She drew in a deep breath as tears welled in her eyes and threatened to break the hold she had so earnestly fought for, "I love you Kane Limaric."

Just a moment longer, she begged her tears which were now flowing freely, please, he's in there...

Slowly, she watched as the raging crimson storm faded from his eyes. Through her own tears, she watched as those red orbs lost their ferocity, to be replaced by a lost, forlorn look. She watched as Kane reemerged, slowly, tentatively, hesitantly, but determined and full of hope. "Sam-" he whispered hoarsely as his dark and familiar eyes gazed into her hazel ones, now filled with tears of relief.

"Kane!" she whispered back as they hugged each other tightly.

Chapter 11

It took a while but soon they and the whole city of Hale and even Green Bay had a fill of what had been happening in Hale. By the third day, it was old news in Green Bay, but not to M'lyka, who could not contain her enthusiasm at the prospects awaiting her with the account Samantha had come back with three days earlier.

"He was ready to die so you could live," M'lyka smiled wistfully. "So true romance does indeed exist!"

"He had surrendered to his pursuers on condition that I would not be next," Samantha shuddered at the memory. "Such is his aversion to loss of human life."

"So, they bit humans to turn them into werewolves, then they would what, experiment on them in search of immortality?"

"Yes, and a cure for their susceptibility to silver." Samantha took a sip of her cocoa. "Five humans died in the process. That was what brought about this whole thing." M'lyka was still not satiated.

"So Kane discovered it while working as a medical research assistant and did not report immediately?"

"He was already too much involved with a human named Elvara, and when his brother confronted him by threatening to expose then, Kane had no choice..."

"My God! Still they killed her- boiled her you said?"

"Yes. Jonah and Kane's uncle Luke- in front of Kane. He's carried a lot of pain with him."

"And now they are dead," M'lyka drew in a sharp breath. "You didn't see the fight?"

"When Nathan, Oloo and Esther came- no. Galou and some others were arrested, but Jonah and Luke tried to fight with the Ethics police. They had no choice, but silver bullets through each.”

“In a house they had turned into a research facility, funded by some woman you said was called Karen?”

“Karen, yeah. Every human had to swear by some god called Nog, I think, according to Rarla, the woman who took me there. Some kind of ceremony... well, Karen was the oldest werewolf in Hale, and the wealthiest. Of course she would have tried to prolong her life, no matter the means.” Samantha stood up as was custom, stepped around clutter on the floor as she headed for the kitchen.

“Well, I’m surprised. All these years we’ve believed that werewolves and humans had no relationships, and now it turns we have so many here in Green Bay who had each of both parents?” M’lyka had followed her into the kitchen. She had a sketchpad in hand and a pencil in the other.

“Well,” Samantha sighed. “Esther, a man they called Oloo, others I have forgotten- the rules are under review as we speak. If society had functioned so far with those among us, then perhaps it is possible.”

“Keep up the hope, Sam. Keep up the hope. Well, I’ll stretch a few canvases and start on these sketches. What do you have planned?”

“Ah, I’m meeting Avenue later. He’s convinced that facing my past about the accident will help me heal.” Samantha sighed. “I’m also meeting with Sarah to see what will come out of speaking civilly to each other will bear.”

“Nothing but goodness Sam, nothing but goodness.” M’lyka smiled. “At least you’re able to mention it.” Samantha smiled back as she stood up and picked her way out. “Healing starts when we face our demons head on.” She walked out, when M’lyka called her.

"Sam," her friend frowned. "Why do all the good adventures seem to happen to you?"

***

She watched him approach. She had noticed him from afar. Why, she didn't know, and she wasn't interested in philosophizing about some random stranger who seemed to be headed her way. She paid no attention to him, though it was obvious that he was most definitely headed her way; he was slowing down as he approached. Sam looked at the dusty footpath he was walking on.

She noticed the small tufts of grass and weeds growing on the path, obstinate and determined, no matter how many times they were trodden on and left misshapen and bent; they still waved when the wind passed by. She looked further off past the approaching stranger and noticed some joggers, silent, panting, determined, just as the trodden weed on the sides of the footpath were.

She next saw a couple; two men passed by, hand in hand, a dog in leash leading them. She looked at the dog briefly; large, floppy ears, docile look. She didn't know the breed. She wasn't that fond of dogs. Even if she was, she couldn't have been interested, not at the moment. She looked at her hands, folded on her lap.

Almost subconsciously, she found herself twirling a strand of dark hair that had escaped from her hastily tied ponytail, just as, unable to pretend that she wasn't interested in the man any longer she looked up, and at the approaching stranger.

"Kane?"

"Yes, Sam?"

"Hold me close. Just hold me and never let go." He moved closer. She yielded herself and he opened his arms, in which she snuggled, her warm breath on his chin as she looked up at him. He looked back at her and the two of them allowed the silence around them to speak for them. No words were needed as the two of them molded themselves into the moment accorded to them by Time, for it had stopped still for them. This was a moment they would forever cherish.

***

"I feel like dancing," she said. She didn't move though. He waited, then carefully extricated himself from her tight but comfy embrace. Walking over to the stereo deck, he pressed its power button. As it lit up and reflected its display in his eyes, he chose input mode and from the neat deck of compact discs, selected one.

A few more presses and turning of knobs, and stereoscopic music filled the room. Letting his mind be overtaken by the emotional tunes, he felt himself carried back to where she was by the melodious, long-drawn violin notes. Every motion was dictated by the music, as he stretched out his hands and she stood up. His eyes did not leave hers as he gathered her into his arms.

Then, the music took over. Their bodies knew and understood. Slowly, unhurriedly, all senses surrendered, the emotive tunes directed every step, every sway, and every caress.

He refused to let his mind take him off the moment. He looked into her eyes as they swayed and sashayed across the floor. Their movements coordinated, their motions fluid, the moment built up- up, till finally, and without words, they both let their feelings loose- letting tentative brushes of their lips speak those feelings out loud. Slowly, their bodies melded and their minds became one. None existed without the other.

***

She snuggled even closer as she caressed his chin.

"I don't know how to describe how I feel," he kissed her lightly, "No words can adequately do justice to my emotions right now."

"Don't try to," she gazed into his eyes. "Words will always limit matters to do with love."

"But the need to express is overwhelming," he whispered.

"Then do it, let it out Kane," she coaxed tenderly. He did. After years, his tears flowed quietly, staining the pillow, the feeling unfamiliar and yet- full of a relief he now realized he had always yearned for. Beside him, she let him express it all, and she listened, quiet, wowed and amazed, and yet at the same time understanding.

THE END